Sniff and
of Spald

They both looked at me as if I'd crawled out from under the log-pile. Tatty and Minta—Fatty and Squinter—I wasn't going to have any problems remembering their names, anyway.

'Some people call me Squinter,' said the one with the gogs, reading my mind. 'Minta the Squinter, see?'

'And some people call me Fatty,' said the other one. 'Tatty the Fatty.'

'But we smash them up if they do,' said Minta. Something told me she wasn't kidding.

Sniff and the Secret of Spalderton Hall

Ian Whybrow

**Illustrated by
Toni Goffe**

RED FOX

A Red Fox Book

Published by Random Century Children's Books
20 Vauxhall Bridge Road, London SW1V 2SA

A division of the Random Century Group

London Melbourne Sydney Auckland
Johannesburg and agencies throughout
the world

First published in 1991 by
The Bodley Head Children's Books

Red Fox edition 1992

1 3 5 7 9 10 8 6 4 2

Printed and bound in Great Britain by
Cox & Wyman Ltd, Reading, Berks

ISBN 0 09 981580 X

One

THUNK! My head smacked against the roof of the car. Next second I was dumped back into my seat and slimed by a corner of Sniff's wet and smelly old blanket. Right in the back of my neck!

Sal was strapped into her safety chair beside me, squeezing chewed Fruit Bar through her fingers. She thought it was all dead funny. 'Do dat adain!' she yelled at Dad.

We were driving along a dirt track through a barley field, towards what looked like a straggly little wood or orchard. The track was no wider than our red Passat Estate. In some places, where the potholes were really mega, someone had dumped rubble, and there was a strip of grass and weeds running along the middle of it that went down like zapped aliens as we bounced forward. Mum was trying to read the Ordnance Survey map. 'Could you slow down a bit, Rob?' she said.

'Can't go much slower without getting stuck,' said Dad. 'But it's OK, I'm sure we're all right. Third left up the lane past the church — once we got into Spalderton. We've done that, so now it's just a question of hanging on.'

Sal grabbed my hair as I was thrown sideways in her direction.

'She's got me again, Mum!' I said.

'Lovely, dear,' said Mum to the map.

'Mum, tell her! She's pulling my hair out,' I said. I got a grip on Sal's disgustingly yucky hand and she let out an ear-piercing scream. Mum rustled the map a bit and told me absent-mindedly to leave Sal alone.

'Right. That's it!' I said. 'I'm calling "Childline" when we get there. I've been abused!'

'Just a sec, Ben,' Mum said, tilting her head on one side to look at the map from a different angle.

We'd been stuck in the back of the car for two and a half hours now. My neck was scratched to pieces, thanks to Sniff. Whenever he got fed up with going round and round on top of the suitcases in the luggage space, trying to bite passing cars, he had a go at climbing over on to the back seat to get a lick at whatever happened to be worth licking on Sal. When he realized that every time he jumped, he got elbowed back to his place by me, he tried to soften me up by hooking his paws on to my collar and pressing his rotten old blanket into my ear. I was well cheesed off.

'Tell you what, old son,' said Dad. 'Not that I want to interfere with your right to turn us over to the authorities or anything, but how'd you fancy driving the rest of the way?'

Good old Dad. He stopped the car and pushed his seat back a few inches to make room for me. Then he tickled Sal to make her laugh so she'd let go of my hair. I opened my door and Sniff abandoned his blanket and dived out into the barley.

'Miff gone!' yelled Sal.

'Don't worry. We're nearly there. He'll be OK,' said Dad. 'Can you see it on the map, babe?'

Mum held the map up and tapped it with her fingernail. 'That's it, definitely,' she said. 'Should be just beyond those trees.'

Dad spread his knees so I could sit down in front of him and steer, while he kept his feet on the pedals. I reached out to turn the keys in the ignition. 'Wait!' said Dad. 'Give me a chance to get the clutch down . . . Right.' I turned the engine over until it caught and Dad revved it up. 'First gear,' he said, and I pushed the lever out of neutral and up to the left.

'Watch out for Sniff,' said Mum, opening her window and peering out. 'Where is he?'

I whistled, and a dark head bobbed up in the barley fifty metres to our left, like a seal coming up from under water.

'He's all right,' I said, getting a firm grip on the steering wheel. Dad lifted his foot. All I had to do was steer — Dad wouldn't let me do the pedals, even off the public road, but it was great — trying to keep the wheels in the dippy ruts and making everyone yell if it looked as if I was going into the barley.

We zigged and zagged for a couple of hundred metres, and when we reached the trees, we saw the red bricks and black beams of the houses for the first time. There were two of them, leaning inwards so that their roofs almost touched in the middle and formed a saggy upside-down W. Something about the way the crooked window frames were set into the walls made you think of eyes, and something about the two front doors made you think of buck teeth. Ivy and other trailing stuff hung round the doors, like a drooping mouth and whiskers. I've never seen a place that looked more like a rabbit.

'Look at that!' said Mum. 'Lavender Cottages. Aren't they marvellous?'

I steered the car off the track into a drive between some apple trees and a boundary hedge of hawthorn.

'Not much sign of lavender,' said Dad. 'But never mind, eh? Plenty of other rural attractions. Just no lavender and no mod cons. Certainly no phone, so bang goes your call to "Childline", old son. Mind you . . . there's always smoke signals.'

'Very funny,' I said.

'Good, though, isn't it? Go on, admit it. It's good really, isn't it?' said Dad.

I personally couldn't see why he and Mum got so excited about this crumbling dump. We were going to be stuck here for a week. Bruno was off in Greece with his mum and dad, Thurston was at 'Disney World' *again*, the jammy so and so. Even Max was going abroad somewhere — staying in some flashy hotel with a swimming pool and disco and everything. I could just imagine what their reaction was going to be when they found out I'd been hanging out at Bugs Bunny Cottages, in the middle of boring Norfolk.

'Someone's been busy, by the look of it,' Dad went on, and you could see that the nettles had been cut down so that we could get the car close to the side of the cottage that had *Number One* painted on the door. Brilliant. The other one had *Number Two* on it. I couldn't think why they bothered.

If the postman ever came here — which I doubted — he was pretty unlikely to think that the first cottage was Number Two unless they counted backwards in these parts.

The pathways that ran round the cottages looked as though they'd recently been cleared too, and there was a small patch of mown grass with three canvas deck-chairs and a bright orange plastic pedal-tractor on it. Everywhere else, the weeds were head-high, and what made it worse, most of the weeds were stinging nettles.

'Germ probably got that gardener chap Morgan from up at the Hall to look in and sort it out for us.'

Germ was a friend of Mum and Dad's from their university days and it was her cottage. Her real name was Germaine but nobody called her that. She didn't exactly *own* the cottage but she'd rented it for years and years ever since she was a student. Mum had told us this story about her while we were driving along:

Germ went to university, and when she got there, she suddenly decided to have a baby. So that meant she had to find somewhere outside the university to live. She bought this old bike and set off one cold February day to look for a cottage. She cycled up and down the country lanes all round North Norfolk and she got more and more cold and tired and depressed because she couldn't find anywhere she could afford. By the time she reached Spalderton village, it was nearly dark and it had started to rain, so she was well knackered and well cheesed off.

Anyway, suddenly this big black car came round the corner with its headlights on and Germ went out of control and fell into a ditch. So there she was, lying in the ditch,

9

soaked, worn out — and pregnant and everything — and the driver of the big car got out and helped her to her feet and asked her if she was OK. She told him about going to have a baby and looking for a place to live and all that, and he said to her, 'Very well, my dear. You shall have one of my cottages. I shall charge you two pounds a week, and don't come crying to me if the roof falls in.' He was Lord Spalderton and he lived at Spalderton Hall. End of story.

Well, nearly. There was a bit more, because Germ had loads more babies after that and she moved to Manchester to work for a newspaper. But she kept the cottage on for weekends and holidays, even though it always looked as if the roof might fall in, and she and her kids went there whenever they could. And good luck to them.

The only trouble was, *this* summer she was going to take them to stay with her sister in Scotland and she said that we could use it, and that we could have it for free if Dad would do some work on the wiring. That's just the sort of thing Dad really likes doing, and Mum's crazy about old houses and stuff — so here we were.

'We'll park just here,' said Dad and I pulled over towards the side of the mown grass and turned off the engine. The electric fan howled for a short while, and when it stopped, all you could hear was the sound of bees.

'Lovely smell,' said Mum when we'd got out and were standing in front of the big old door. 'What are those? They're everywhere.'

'Daisies,' I said.

'Not those. They're marguerites, anyway. No, those.' She

pointed to a clump of tall plants with juicy stems that looked as though they had been extended in sections like massive, wonky car aerials and were covered in pinkish-purply dangling flowers. Big fat bees kept dive-bombing into them.

'Slipper orchids?' said Dad.

'Come off it, Dad!' I said. 'They're some kind of weed. But they do smell nice — like jam.'

'Something balm, I think,' said Mum, giving Sal a tug to save her from the bee she was trying to grab from inside one of the flowers. 'Not a good idea, Sal. Come on, let's have a look inside, shall we?' Sal immediately ran the other way and bbbrrmmmed the orange pedal-tractor round the grass.

' 'Smine!' she said to me, just because I was looking at her. 'You shut up, bum-bum, cos I can brrrm dis.'

'What about next door?' said Dad. He pushed through the overgrown flower-bed in front of next door's window and put his face up to the glass. 'No sign of life. No one staying there at the moment. Great! That means we're in for a really peaceful time.'

Mum took this massive key out of her bag, like a key for a church door. She slotted it into the keyhole of Number One. Heave, click. Then she turned the doorknob and shoved. Nothing happened. Dad stepped across, grabbed the door-knob and heaved his shoulder against the wood. The door gave a groan and shuddered open. Dad ducked under the purple flowers and ivy that hung down over the door frame and stepped in.

We followed him into the cool, dark, earthy room. It was too low for Dad to stand up straight in, unless he stood with his head between two of the rough beams. The floor was just sort of uneven paving stones. There was a huge, squashy sofa and armchair. There were books everywhere, piled up in heaps and crammed on to shelves. On every surface where there weren't books, there were signs of the seaside or the country . . . shells, stones, pebbles, dried seaweed, a snorkel and face mask, two odd flippers, great bunches of teasels and rushes, and dead daisies in jam-jars and brown pots. There was a portable TV on a wormy old table. It was black and white and probably clockwork. No sign of a video or anything. Under the stairs that went up steeply in the corner beside the big brick fireplace was an old record player and piles of faded old LPs. On the far side of the room was a narrow door that led to the kitchen.

'Ah, this is one of the fittings that needs replacing,' said Dad. He flicked the ancient light switch and you could hear it fizz as the weak light flickered above the vast old kitchen table. 'And that's your job, Ben, old son,' he said, nodding towards the old black stove squatting in the corner. 'If we want hot water, we'll have to get that going. Let's have a look out here.'

He opened the back door, and we peered out into a jungle of tall weeds and flowers, bushes and fruit trees. Under a collapsing lean-to, there were loads of logs, many of them green with moss and lichen. I lifted one of the bottom ones with my foot. It was so rotten it broke off like wet Shredded Wheat, and a huge toad with yellow leaf-shaped markings flopped out. Well, that was something interesting, anyway. Sal had come through the house to the back, dragging the tractor behind her. She dumped the tractor and grabbed the poor toad before it had a chance to get back under the log-pile. It kicked and squirmed but she held on tight, so it did a yellow squirt on her. That made her let go all right, and the toad lolloped off out of harm's way. Sal looked closely at the gunk on the palm of her hand. Just for a second, I thought she was going to lick it, but she suddenly changed her mind and rubbed it off on her dress. She squatted down to see if there was anything else interesting under the woodpile.

'I'm going to have a look upstairs,' I said, ducking back inside. I ran through the kitchen, pausing just long enough to have a dekko into the musty old pantry, and turned up the winding stairs.

There seemed to be four rooms. The three I could see into were each painted a different bright colour and covered with drawings and paintings done by little kids, and proper ones as well with sailing ships and ladies with no clothes on. The low ceilings sloped from the back to the front and made you feel you were falling, and they bulged downwards, specially in the big room.

'Doesn't look too safe,' Mum said to Dad. They were standing behind me and she was looking decidedly anxious.

'I shouldn't let it worry you. They've obviously held up for about four hundred years,' said Dad. 'Hey, this is great!' He threw himself on the huge brass bed that twanged and boinged under his weight. 'Bags this one for Mum and me. Which one are you going for, old son?'

There was one door I hadn't tried, at the back of the cottage, so I nipped along to try it now. You had to go up three steps to it and it was really low and crooked. I flipped the latch and the door fell open by itself. I ducked inside.

It was dead good, like a big cupboard, with loads of

interesting junk in it. And there were these really solid hand-built bunk beds, painted blue, and from the top one you could look through a round window that had been cut into the thick wall. There was a blue chest and a blue wardrobe. And there were loads of blue shelves piled high with books and boxes of games — and plenty of *Dungeons and Dragons* manuals, too. And some pretty good posters, I noticed, with First World War Weapons, Champion Racing Cars and Fighting Ships. There was a record deck that looked OK and one empty shelf that seemed to be set up for a computer and printer. Whoever generally used the room was obviously pretty interesting, so, when Mum and Dad looked in and saw me curled up in the round window space, they guessed right: I'd bagged this room for myself.

'Good view?' Dad said, coming over and peering out at the jungle of the back garden. I was looking straight down at the wall that had ivy and wisteria climbing up it.

'Great,' I said. 'Where's the bathroom?' I swung round and out of the window space.

'Haven't seen it so far,' Dad said. 'Keep looking. I'd better go and make sure Sal's not swallowing frogs or anything.'

Mum and I clattered downstairs behind him and we found Sal still poking about with a stick under the log-pile.

'Found anything exciting?' said Dad, and then noticed the four snails she'd stuck on one arm, and the ginormous yellow slug which was clinging on to the other, waving the stalks of its eyes about.

'Dey tickle,' she said.

'Well, shall we just put them back where we found them?'

said Mum, looking a bit strained.

'Let's see where this goes,' I said, starting along the well-trodden pathway that led to the boundary hedgerow at the back. I picked my way carefully, stepping over brambles, treading down stray nettles and warning Sal to mind them, until we came to a little brick hut. I flicked the latch, pulled the door open and peered into the gloom. There was this horrible disinfectant smell and the sound of fizzing blue-bottles. Then, as your eyes got used to the dark, you could make out a wooden frame with a loo seat set into it and a white bucket underneath. 'Yuck!' I said.

Dad laughed. 'What did you expect? We're miles away from a main drainage system here. But it's clean enough and practical, and I'm sure somebody comes and empties the bucket. If not, you and I'll have to form a burial party once a week.'

'You must be joking!' I said. 'I'm not going in there!'

Sal didn't mind, of course. She'd already decided that it was just her sort of place. She insisted on Mum lifting her on the seat for a try-out. That was it. She was hooked.

By now, Sniff had joined us again. He was covered in sticky-buds. He didn't care, though, and he didn't seem to mind about nettles. He was shivering with excitement and dived into the hut. You could tell *he* was going to enjoy himself, anyway.

It didn't take long before Sal had got stung all over, so Dad took her indoors to administer some soothing lotion while Mum went to sort out the stuff from the car. She said she'd rather get on without me and Sniff getting under her feet, so we carried on exploring round the back.

There were plum and apple trees everywhere — so that was something. The plums on the lower branches were dead wincy, but when I climbed high enough, I found softer, juicier ones that the sun had got to. They were good — warm and sweet — and the kind that didn't have stringy bits that get stuck between your front teeth. I spat the stones into the weeds below and Sniff went chasing in after them. I made a note of where the clusters of ripe plums were, so that I could come back with a carrier bag later. Then I stuffed a few in my pockets, climbed down and headed for the tallest tree in sight.

As far as fruit went, this tree didn't look very promising at first but I thought it would make a good lookout post. I heaved myself up and hooked my feet round the lowest branch and could see one or two yellowy blobs of fruit way up among the highest branches — greengages. Dead twigs snapped off against my shoulders and pattered down as I struggled upwards, feeling with my feet and hands for the strongest holds. I had just reached the sweeter, juiciest fruit when I heard the sound of a motorbike engine. Sniff heard it, too, and suddenly he was crashing through the undergrowth towards the drive at the side of the cottage.

That was when I realized what a great view there was from the top of this greengage tree. Beyond the overgrown hedges that went right round the cottages, the barley was moving in waves, just like the sea. Looking away from the house and over a little rise, you could see the round stone tower of the church in Spalderton village. The other way, and there was the little round window of my room, and between the slopes of the roofs of Lavender Cottages, over another field — of what might have been wheat — there was a long, winding stone wall and sheep grazing under the trees behind it. Far beyond that, you could see the grey roof, yellow stone walls and flashing windows of what I guessed was Spalderton Hall, where Lord Spalderton, Germ's landlord, lived.

I shifted position, easing myself up to a branch that looked safe to sit on, and looked down between my knees at the orchard. Way over in the far corner was a little brick building — probably the other cottage's outside loo – and almost. hidden in a tangle of trees, bushes and nettles, against the boundary hedge on the far side of our loo, was the peeling white roof of an old caravan. It was so well covered, you couldn't have seen it from ground level. I made a mental note to hack out a path to it through the nettles.

The motorbike noise was suddenly getting a lot louder, and as I twisted round to look, I was just in time to catch a glimpse of Sniff racing towards it along the dirt track. If there was a motorbike in the lane, he was certainly not going to let it go by without having a bark at it.

Two

Sniff was racing along the track through the barley like a rocket, with dust waving up behind him like a vapour trail. He almost reached the lane and then — wipeout! He tried to brake and U-turn at the same time as the massive great motorbike and sidecar came thundering straight at him.

BLAM! The thing backfired like a bazooka. Sniff rolled over a few times, his tail between his legs, and spurted for cover into the barley. Behind the driver, the two passengers, one on the pillion and the other in the sidecar, raised their fists and punched the air.

I was off my branch and down that tree so fast, I skinned my hands and tore a lump out of the seat of my jeans. I thrashed through the nettles, keeping my hands above my head and ducking quickly back on to the path to avoid them altogether whenever I could. I zoomed down the side of our cottage, playing a cavalry charge in my head — bap-buddap-buddap-buddah! I wasn't sure what I was going to do to hold a gang of Hell's Angels off, but I reckoned that a few well-aimed plums and greengages might be enough to confuse them until Dad arrived and sorted them out. Or maybe Sniff would come out of hiding and scare them away.

As I ran round the corner where Mum was unpacking things from the car, I saw her look up, shocked to see that we were being invaded by three leather-jacketed greebos on a motorbike and sidecar. The driver was wearing an old-fashioned leather helmet like a pudding basin with leather flaps for the ears, goggles with evil yellow glass in them like a dispatch rider's in a war film, a brown leather flying jacket, the kind with a woolly lining, and a white scarf tucked in at the neck. The two passengers wore big, flashy fibreglass helmets with visors that snapped down on to jutting-out chin guards. Their black leather bikers' jackets were identical, with fancy crisscross padding on the shoulders and elbows.

The driver switched off the engine and dismounted, and it was a bit of a relief to see Dad standing in the doorway. I didn't stand much of a chance against this lot, armed with just a pocketful of soft fruit, and I was still bashing my brains, trying to think of some other really smart way of dealing with the situation, when the passengers threw two beaten-up old canvas bags on to the grass and stood up in the sidecar so that its springs twanged like a bed.

The driver started towards Mum. He wasn't tall, just evil-looking, his leather pants creaking and boot-buckles jingling.

'Hello, I'm Lolly.' The voice, surprisingly posh, was a woman's. She had taken off her glove and you could see that her nails were painted silver. She held out one hand to Mum and undid the straps of her helmet with the other. 'And may I introduce my daughters, Tatty and Minta?'

Tatty and Minta? *Daughters?* They took off their helmets

and rested them on the pillion of the bike. Their hair was straight and quite short, more punked up than their mum's, the same dark colour but streaked with orange bits. They had round, angry faces with deep dimples in their cheeks and chins, wide mouths and squidgy noses. And they were exactly the same, exactly, in every detail . . . twins, probably about my age or a bit older. The one in the sidecar climbed out, reached into a little pocket in the interior, took out a pair of round, wire-framed glasses and hooked them over her ears. The other girl didn't seem to need glasses. They both looked at me as if I'd crawled out from under the log-pile. Tatty and Minta — Fatty and Squinter — I wasn't going to have any problems remembering their names, anyway.

'Some people call me Squinter,' said the one with the gogs, reading my mind. 'Minta the Squinter, see?'

'And some people call me Fatty,' said the other one. 'Tatty the Fatty.'

'But we smash them up if they do,' said Minta. Something told me she wasn't kidding.

'It's been a bit of a hassle for them,' Lolly explained. 'We've done a runner on George, their dad. Shall I show you why?' She lifted her goggles and displayed a really ace black eye. It went from purple to green underneath and the white was all bloodshot.

'He's a poet,' said Tatty. 'He thumped her.'

'The swine!' said Mum.

'Just because he's dried up,' said Lolly. 'Hasn't written a thing for months.'

'What, writer's block, you mean?' asked Dad.

'Right!' said Lolly. 'A real bummer for him but I mean to say . . .'

'No need for violence,' said Mum.

'Right!' said Lolly. 'And right out of the blue like that.'

'Wham!' said Minta, throwing a punch to demonstrate.

'Blam!' said Tatty, kicking the heads off a couple of weeds.

'So we decided to split,' said Lolly. 'Because I mean, he'd really *flipped* . . .'

'He tried to follow us and we had to lose him,' went on Minta.

'That meant driving miles in the wrong direction to put him off the scent,' said Lolly. 'Anyway, we made it, in spite of the fact that the timing's gone haywire on the bike and it's backfiring a bit. And it looks as if we've rather put the wind up your dog. Sorry about that.' Sniff was cowering behind Dad.

Lolly suddenly realized something, and pointed at Mum and Dad. 'Hey! Wait a sec! Don't I know you?' she said. 'You're friends of Germ's, aren't you? You won't remember me, but I was the year below you at university, on the Fine Arts course. I dropped out when I met my first husband. So you two are still together after all this time. How romantic!'

Mum and Dad blushed.

'We've decided to lie low in Kev's cottage — just until the heat's off,' Lolly went on, jerking her thumb at Number Two to indicate that it was Kev's — whoever he was. 'Wow, we're going to have *heaps* to rap about! Isn't it great here? I haven't been for years but it hasn't changed at all. It's gorgeous.' She closed her eyes, took a deep breath, and held it in her lungs for a while as if she were testing it for quality. She breathed out noisily, nodded her head once with satisfaction and asked, 'What's Germ up to at the moment?'

Mum told her about Germ going to Scotland, explained how we'd just arrived and asked if they fancied a cup of tea — if they could find a kettle to boil. Lolly said that would be really cool and behind her, Tatty and Minta started nudging each other, giggling and pointing at the rip in my jeans.

'You can see his bum,' one of them said, which I thought was dead rude.

Boy, this crowd turning up really put the mockers on the holiday — and just when I was beginning to think that this place had one or two things going for it.

Three

Sniff doesn't usually lose his bottle — not because of motorbikes anyway. It was probably just the backfiring that gave him the heebie-jeebies, and that was understandable — but he was obviously embarrassed. He crept in the back door and lay under the kitchen table while the rest of us had tea in the front room. Tatty and Minta sat on the squashy sofa and scowled and made sarky comments, while I made my tea last for as long as I could so that I didn't have to say anything. I would have liked another slice of banana bread. Next to her carrot cake, it's the best thing Mum makes. This was really juicy, with crunchy walnut bits in it — but I only got a titchy little chunk and Ugly and Wuggly scoffed the rest of the plateful in about ten seconds. So there was nothing for me to do except pretend I was dead interested in Germ's books.

I had a flick through *A Petrological Study of Certain Iron Age Pottery in Eastern England*. The most interesting thing about that was the moth that had got squashed between page 488 and page 489. Then there was this one called *Paul Klee: a Monograph*, which had loads of drawings that reminded me of the stuff Wilmslow scribbles on his sportsbag. There were loads of cookery books — *Cooking with Nettles* and *Eat Yourself into a Better Person* — the kind of thing that Mum goes in for. Mostly it was stuff like *The Parent and the Potty* and *A Hundred and One Reasons Why Baby Won't Sleep*. Germ really went in for babies.

'Smelly in here, isn't it?' said Tatty, loudly enough for me to hear it through the conversation Mum and Dad were having with Lolly about their university days.

'Probably those books,' said Minta.

'Or him.'

'Or him.'

I didn't look up to see whether it was Sniff or me they were insulting. It was probably both. Anyway, Sniff thought they were talking about him, because he started thumping his tail on the floor and panting. He got up off his old jersey and dragged it through the doorway and over to the sofa. What a crawler! He'd do anything for a tug of war.

Rrr-rrr-rrr-rrr! Sniff huffed and growled and bunched up his shoulders and pulled as if he and the twins were old chums. They waited until he was bracing himself for a really strong pull and then let go. Sniff shot backwards like something out of a catapult and whammed into one of the brown jars with bulrushes in. It smashed on the flagstones by the stairs.

'That dog's as stupid as it looks,' said Tatty, while Sniff slunk off, feeling dafter than ever.

'Silly boy!' said Mum, who had been too caught up in her memories of the old days to see what had happened. She bent to pick up the broken pieces of pot and the scattered rushes.

'Like him,' said Minta, meaning me.

Sal, who had been in the kitchen, busily occupied with her own personal plate of banana bread, toddled in and stamped on the bulrushes until Dad hoisted her out of the way.

'Look what you've done, you barmy beast!' Dad said to Sniff. 'You take your jersey out into the garden. Go on. Buzz off.' He opened the back door. 'Shoo! Out!'

'Shoo, out!' Sal joined in.

'Ben,' said Dad, 'come and get a dustpan and brush — I saw one in the kitchen cupboard — and help Mum sweep this lot up.' He turned to Tatty and Minta, who were sitting looking as if butter wouldn't melt. 'All right, girls? Ben looking after you?'

'Ah,' said Mum standing up, her arms full of bulrushes, 'those poor girls are looking totally neglected. I see all the banana bread has gone. Ben, I expect. He's a glutton for banana bread. Ben, dear, come and get some more for your guests. You can do the sweeping-up afterwards. More tea, girls? Ben'll be happy to get you a refill . . . Come on, Ben, the poor things are gasping.'

Tatty and Minta held out their mugs for me and smiled stupid smirky smiles and blinked about nine billion times to show how much they were enjoying having me run around.

They polished off the next plate of banana bread before I'd finished clearing up the mess of brown jar and bulrushes. I looked up to see the twins leaning back on the sofa, slurping their tea with their little fingers crooked, taking the mickey.

'Doesn't say much, does it?'

'No, it doesn't.'

'Makes a nice little housemaid, though.'

'What sort of stuff does your dad write?' I asked. I just threw it in. It made them stop and look at each other.

'He's a poet. He's artistic.'

'Yeah, but what sort of poems does he write?' I asked.

'About Nature.'

'Want to hear one?'

'If you like,' I said.

They said it together:

> 'Roses are red
> Violets are blue
> You've got a face
> Like elephant poo.'

They laughed and laughed until they coughed, and then they coughed and coughed until they started to go blue. Then they got out two little spray things and puffed them into their mouths and breathed in hard.

'We've got asthma,' Minta wheezed, as though she thought I wished I had it. 'Tat like nearly died of it last summer, din't you, Tat?'

'Can you fight?' Tatty said.

'Why?' I said. I thought it was probably a trick question.

'Sacha and Rupert are always fighting but we can beat them in, can't we, Minta?'

'Every time,' said Minta.

'Who are Rupert and Sacha?' I asked, thinking *poor guys*.

'Our stepbrothers, from Mum's first marriage,' Tatty said. 'They're older than us.'

'Well, they would be,' I said, 'if your mum had them before she had you.'

26

Tatty and Minta looked at each other, raised their eyebrows, nodded in agreement and moved in. They were obviously going to belt the daylights out of me. I started backing towards the stairs, thinking maybe there was somewhere upstairs I could lock myself in . . .

Luckily, Lolly stepped in to save me. It was time for them to get settled in next door. 'Having a good time, you guys?' she asked. 'Sorry. Got to tear you away. You can get together with Ben again later. Come and grab your bags, will you?' She opened the front door and waved the twins through it.

Mum, Dad and I stood in the doorway and watched them. Sniff had come round to the front. As our visitors stepped on to the grass, he was just lifting his leg and peeing against the spokes of the wheel of the sidecar. The pee made a kind of chiming noise. Tatty and Minta ran at him. He ducked down, grabbed the handle of one of the canvas bags that were lying nearby and tugged it along the ground.

'Just ignore him,' Dad called. 'Otherwise he'll think you want to play.'

Meanwhile, Lolly was kick-starting the bike. It backfired twice and made us all jump. Sniff did a double somersault and dropped the bag, and Tatty and Minta thought it was so hilarious they had to punch each other. Then they turned and pointed at me standing with my hands over my ears and laughed their heads off. Lolly rode the bike out of sight round the other side of the cottages.

Sniff cowered under the hedge for a moment, but when he saw Tatty and Minta pointing at me, he must have thought it was a signal to go fetch or something, because in spite of the noise the bike was making, he got his nerve back, darted out, swiped the bag and made a run for it towards the orchard at the back.

Tatty and Minta threw themselves at him in a double flying tackle. But they missed. Sniff was too quick for them. He darted back for a second to wind them up, and then shot off again. They were on their feet surprisingly quickly for their size, and tearing down the path after Sniff. They were out of sight in a second and shouting with fury.

Go it, Sniffo! I said to myself. *Bury the thing!*

And it wasn't long before the angry shouts changed into squeaks and yells of pain. Sniff must have led them into the head-high stingers.

Nice one, Sniff, I thought, trotting inside for a good private chuckle to myself. *Nice one*.

The little bottle of calamine lotion that Dad had dabbed on Sal's stings earlier was on the mantelpiece. I hid it behind a postcard and went in search of a slice of banana bread.

Four

'Those poor girls are still covered in blotches, even this morning,' Dad was saying, the following day. 'It was really stupid of me to forget what I did with that calamine — it seemed to do the trick for Sal.'

He was pouring two-stroke mixture into the beaten-up old Flymo he'd found amongst the rest of the junk in the outhouse, which stood between the cottages at the back. I was standing in the doorway with a bucketful of logs for the boiler. I put the bucket down and had a good look at the junk.

Most of the room was taken up by a ladder, and a heap of rusty bikes, one of them with the front wheel smaller than the back one and a frame over the front wheel big enough to hold an apple box. It was an old-fashioned butcher's bike, which they used ages ago for deliveries. Dad suggested we might have a crack at getting it roadworthy when we'd cleared some more nettles.

I walked to the other end of the outhouse and looked through the door into what was laughingly called the bathroom. When the cottages were first built, there must have been a narrow alleyway between them. At some time, the front entrance had been bricked up and somebody had put a corrugated iron roof over the alley, turning the long, narrow space into an extra room, with a door leading into it from the back garden. Then it was turned into two rooms, with a partition in the middle. One half was the bathroom, and the other half the outhouse — an extra room for putting junk in.

The bathroom had a brick floor and a ginormous cast-iron bath with great big clawed feet. The pipe connected to the huge, rusty tap that said COLD came out of the wall of Number Two and the pipe for the tap that said HOT came out through the wall of our cottage.

'Dad,' I said. 'Has anybody had a bath yet?'

'Not as far as I know. Why?'

'Do you realize that the hot-water pipe comes through from our side?'

'Uh-huh. Germ told me.'

'Is there another bath — in the other cottage?'

'Nope. This has to do for both. No wonder people only live here during the summer, eh? Dear oh dear, you'd have to be in a desperate state to take a bath in the winter.'

'So how come I have to slave away keeping our boiler going for next door to have baths?'

'For one thing, you like fires. For another thing, it's a nice little responsibility for you. And thirdly, there's a special agreement with Kevin, the bloke who rents Number Two. Germ keeps the boiler going, so he collects most of the wood and saws it up and stacks it. He's got a permit to go into

30

Foxton Wood and clear dead trees in winter. I expect he's got a chain-saw somewhere. See? The bloke next door does the hard part.'

'Still means I have to get up early and clean out the stove and chuck out the ashes and fetch in piles of logs and relight the fire — and Fatty and Squinter don't have to do anything.'

'You'd better not let your mother hear you calling them that,' Dad said. You could tell he thought it was funny, though, because he turned away quickly so I wouldn't catch him smiling. 'And anyway — they've had a rough life by the sound of it. Their dad sounds like a real thug.'

'What will you do if he turns up here, Dad?'

Dad looked thoughtful. 'Shouldn't think he will,' he said, after a while. 'He probably doesn't even know this place exists.'

'Yeah, but if he does . . . what are you going to do?'

Dad scratched his chin and streaked oil across his beard. 'Let's cross that bridge when we get to it, old son.'

'He might whack Lolly again, mightn't he?' I wanted to hear Dad say he would sort him out, give him a hammering. There weren't any phones in the cottages, so nobody could call the police without going down to the village, and by then it would probably be too late . . .

'I doubt it,' said Dad. 'But we'll play it by ear.' He started rummaging through his tool-box. 'Anyway . . . one job at a time.'

I peered round at the bath again. Laid on top of it was a sheet of corrugated fibreglass and one of those slatted wooden duckboards they have on the floors in swimming pool changing rooms. There was crooked wooden shelf fixed to the wall, with a plastic duck on it, and a tugboat and a clockwork frog with a broken leg, and a wooden nesting box — one of those things that looks like a little house, with a sloping roof and hole in one of the end walls.

On the opposite wall, there was a row of old-fashioned coat hooks — like they have in old school buildings — so you had somewhere to hang your togs while you were in the tub. Dead luxurious, the coat hooks.

All of a sudden there was a whirring sound. Something darted over my head, through the bathroom door, on through the outhouse, past Dad, and out into the sunshine.

'What was *that*?' I yelled.

Dad grinned. 'A swift by the look of it. Or a martin. There must be a nest in there.'

I had a look. Actually, there were two nests built against the wall and under the edge of the corrugated iron roof of the bathroom. They were a bit too neat and rounded for swifts, I reckoned, but they were similar, made of mud and almost closed, with a little entrance at the top. There were droppings all over the place, 'specially directly underneath the nests, where there were two speckly heaps of the stuff. That explained why there was a cover over the bath.

Dad was standing behind me now, looking into the bathroom. 'Martins, definitely,' he said. 'Mucky little devils, aren't they?' He smiled. 'Maybe somebody was thinking of hanging up the nesting box for them — but they prefer good old honest-to-goodness mud, obviously.' He suddenly remembered something and held up his forefinger: ' "Where they most breed and haunt, I have observed the air is delicate." What d'you reckon, old son?' he asked, grinning. He took a good long sniff and wrinkled up his nose.

'What?'

'Shakespeare,' said Dad. 'Talking about martins. How about that! Mind you, it's about the only bit I can remember from *Macbeth* apart from "Down, Spot, down." That's Lady Macbeth, that bit, I think.'

'Did she have a Dalmatian?'

'Must have done,' said Dad. 'It's been a heck of a long time since I studied it. Anyway, come on. Let's see if we can get this Flymo going.'

It started after a couple of tries, and Dad jerked forward, up the track towards the loo. Chewed nettle stalk, weeds and grasses splashed out over his feet. He steadied himself and pressed forward, swinging the cutter out to left and right, higher and higher, bashing at the uncut stuff that had grown tall at the sides. Every time he swung it up, the engine note changed from a low growl to a rattling whine. By the time he got to the end of the path and was banging the rim of the Flymo against the brick step of the loo, the sweat was running into Dad's eyes.

'Tough going!' he yelled. 'More of a problem than I thought, to deal with the tall stuff. I don't think you'd better try. It'll be too heavy for you, especially the way the mown stuff sticks to the casing.'

I was disappointed. I imagined how great it must feel to have the power to make the weeds sort of melt out of your way in neat strips like a combine harvester slicing the edge off a solid wall of wheat. Not that that was how it looked when Dad did it. It was all pretty ragged, except along the path that had been cut before. Suddenly, I noticed that Dad was looking straight past me. I turned and nearly jumped out of my skin. Staring at us round the side of the cottage, his face partly shadowed by his battered straw hat, was this tough-looking bloke . . .

Even from this distance, you could see he was big. He wasn't any taller than Dad but he was broader. He tipped his hat further down over his face to shade his eyes from the sun and get a better look at us.

I felt really sick, all of a sudden. It was him, George — Lolly's husband! He must have guessed where she was hiding out, and here he was, come to get her. There was no telling what he'd do to her if he got his hands on her again!

When he saw Dad and me gawping back at him, he started to come down the path towards us — and for a big bloke, he was moving fast.

Five

Dad had turned right round now and I hopped out of the way
to stand beside him as he swung the Flymo back on to the
path between us and the hurrying stranger.

As he came nearer, I studied him carefully. I was thinking
about giving a description to the police if I had to make a run
for it to the village.

Tallish, with a bit of a stoop.
Heavily built. Big hands.
Age: Hard to tell, Fiftyish?
Face: sunburnt nose, cheeks and chin. Bushy grey
moustache going right across to the ears with fluffy bits
sticking out halfway up his cheeks.
Eyes: small and very pale blue.
Bushy eyebrows.
Wearing an old straw hat with a black band, a striped blue
and white shirt with no collar, a tweed jacket, and brown
cord trousers held up by a thick brown belt. Heavy brown
boots.
Occupation: poet

So that's what poets looked like.

He had to shout to be heard over the noise of the Flymo. He touched the side of his hat with his finger. 'Got it goin', then? Meks yer sweat, eh?' he said to Dad.

Dad cut the engine and wrestled with the machine for a few seconds while it shuddered to a stop. 'Mr Morgan?' he said, holding out his hand.

Mr Morgan? The gardener from Spalderton Hall! Not the Mad Poet after all!

'That's roight. Got it in one,' said Mr Morgan. 'Miss Germaine said yer was comin' so I med a start on clearin' the paths. 'Fraid I got a lot to do up 'is Lordship's place at the moment, so I can't do no more. But I'll tell yer what, yer got the wrong boy for the job there.'

'What, Ben?' said Dad.

'Lord, no! Not this li'l ol' boy, no! I'm talkin' about that ol' Flymo yer got there. 'Tain't no good for tall nettles an' such.'

'What do you suggest, then?' asked Dad.

Mr Morgan winked at me. 'You bring your dadda along with me, boy. We'll hev a look in me ol' wagon. I'll see you roight.'

He took us round to the front, to where an old green Morris Traveller was parked behind our Passat. Mr Morgan patted its roof and ran his finger along one of the varnished wooden window frames. 'Don't see many cars nowadays what's got a touch of the ol' woodworm, do you?' he said with another wink. 'But she's a goer, she can still go all roight. Now then . . .'

Mr Morgan opened the double doors at the back and lifted

some sacking, to reveal two long, curved, white wooden handles.

'Know what them two are?'

'Scythes?' said Dad.

'Them's the boys!' said Mr Morgan. 'Them's what you want. I'll lend yer a couple.'

'Don't think we could manage those properly,' said Dad. 'Us townies.'

'Won't tek long to teach yer. Like to hev a go?'

'That'd be something, eh, Ben?' said Dad, who could see I was as keen as he was. 'As you say, that old Flymo is obviously not the best tool for the job so . . . if you can spare the time, we'd love to have a bash.'

'Thet's the spirit! Thet's what I like to hear. Well, get hold of thet one, boy, and I'll put out this bigger chappy for yer dadda. They won't hurt yer with the sackin' on.'

We went over to the patch of cut grass by the front of the cottages and took the sacking off. The blades were wicked, much longer than I thought and curving to a point. I felt a bit nervous and Mr Morgan was quick to notice.

'Yep, he'll bite yer! Thet'd tek yer foot clean off, so yer got to handle it roight. Yer don't want to go swingin' at yer job.' He stepped to the edge of the grass, facing a line of cow parsley, and showed us how it was done. It was like magic; with a slight fizz, the row of cow parsley came toppling down in a gentle wave.

'There yer go. Now hev a shot yerselves.'

Dad and I were useless at first, but with Mr Morgan's help, we soon got the hang of it.

'Thet's the stuff!' said Mr Morgan. 'There now, soon as I

seen yer, I thought them's the fellers to learn a trade! I knowed thet when I heard yer got thet ol' Flymo started. Teks a bit of doin', thet do!'

Mr Morgan really knew how to make you feel good. Dad and I grinned at him.

'Now I've got to get along to the ol' Hall, look, so I'll leave yer to get on with it. I'll drop by tomorrow mornin' and see how yer gettin' on. Don't forget to put the sackin' on them blades and put 'em well outa the way when yer finished.'

'Don't worry,' said Dad. 'We'll parcel them up nice and tight. You're sure you're happy about lending them to us?'

'Thet's a dyin' art, thet is. When I was a lad here, I used to mow near on two acres a day, come the harvest. Not now, o' course, but . . . well, give me a bit of a glow to pass on some of the ol' ways. They'll be gone before yer knows it. But don't go cuttin' down that wood calamint what grow up against the cottages. Thet's bootiful, thet is, and thet's rare! Yer won't find thet growin' many other places 'cept for the Isle Of Wight.'

'Wood calamint. Not some kind of *balm*, eh?' said Dad.

'No, balm's whiter. Flowers earlier, too,' said Mr Morgan, and he set òff at his usual fast pace towards his 'wagon'. 'Mind how yer go, boys!' he called as he jumped in.

Before his old Morris had bounced its way to the end of the track, Dad and I were hard at it. I was working among the tall grasses, making a bigger lawn at the front and Dad was happily ripping down the nettles to widen the paths. It was . . . Thurston would have a word for it. Fantasticuloso? Tremenderistic? Anyway, it felt really good, pulling behind the dry stalks and watching lines of grass sort of faint and tumble to one side like a human wave. I was thinking that there probably weren't any other kids in England who knew how to mow the old-fashioned way.

Six

By the time Mum, Sal, Lolly, Tatty and Minta — and Sniff, of course — had got back from their trip to the village, Dad and I had done an amazing job. The front lawn was miles bigger, you could walk right round the cottages in shorts if you wanted to, you could get to the trees with the best fruit without getting stung to death. *Plus*, we'd found some interesting stuff, too — four tennis balls, a shuttlecock, a cup and saucer, a silver spoon, a wellington boot, an egg-beater and a golf club; not to mention loads of frogs and toads, two harvest mice, a teeny shrew, and loads of different kinds of butterflies and moths.

My best find was a coronation tea caddy with four different keys in it. The tea caddy wasn't all that rusty, so it can't have been outdoors for very long. It crossed my mind when I was thinking about the keys — maybe one of them was for the old caravan.

Dad found something really ace as well.

I was slightly cheesed off at not being allowed to demonstrate to everybody what an ace mower I was but Dad said that Sal or Sniff could get hurt with sharp edges like that around . . . so, fair enough — better to stash the scythes out of the way until Mr Morgan collected them in the morning. Anyway, I had a heap of goodies to show people, including the thing Dad had found and the harvest mouse that I'd stuck into my shirt pocket to scare Tatty and Minta with.

'What d'you reckon, old son?' Dad asked, turning over the thing he'd found in his hands.

'Where'd you find it?'

'Right over the other side of Number Two, under the hedge near the path.'

'Looks like a grappling iron,' I said, feeling a bit weird all of a sudden because it reminded me of a little adventure I'd had with Max and Thurston with a hook on the end of Max's mother's washing line.

'Dead right,' said Dad. 'That's what I thought. Beautifully made, isn't it? Cast iron. Very likely done by a blacksmith. D'you know what I think it's for?'

'I should think you tie a rope on to that ring and bung it up over a castle wall so you can climb up.'

'You could do, but I don't reckon so in this case. I reckon this is for fishing buckets out of a well.'

'What, here?'

'Could easily be. We haven't cleared away all the weeds and stuff by a long shot, so there could easily be a well in the undergrowth. After all, these cottages have been here for centuries, so whoever lived in them must have got their water from somewhere before they got it piped in. My guess is it's probably been filled in or bricked over. Anyway, talking of piping in water, I'm all mucky and sweaty and so are you . . . I think what we need is a quick bath before the rest of the gang gets back. Give me a hand with this, will you?' He got hold of one end of the corrugated bath cover.

'Oh, Dad, not with the martins and everything! It's horrible!'

'Don't be such a wimp!' said Dad. 'A little bit of bird-poop never hurt anyone. You run the water, I'll get the towels and some soap.' We stood the cover against the wall, put the wooden duckboard on the brick floor, and I leaned over and turned on the tap marked HOT. It spluttered a bit, and the pipe banged against the wall, but it worked: hot water started coming out of it.

As it turned out, there was no need to worry about getting dive-bombed by the residents — the parent martins had the sense to buzz off when the pipes started rattling, though they did flit back to feed the chicks once we were in the tub. No, when the attack came, it wasn't from the air.

Whoever built this crazy bathroom had never bothered to put a lock on the door. Even if they had, it wouldn't have made any difference because the frame had warped and you couldn't shut the door properly anyway. Dad said it would be OK if we whistled. So there we were, sitting in the bath, whistling away, trying out the tugboat and the clockwork frog with one leg, when everybody turned up. When I say *everybody*, what I mean is, Sal turned up first. Having walked back from the village, Mum had put the kettle on and sent Sal out to look for us to see if we wanted a cup of tea or something.

Sal stood on her toes on the duckboard with her chin on the edge of the bath and peered in.

'Do you mind?' I said.

'Hello, Sal,' said Dad. 'Had a nice walk? And a lollipop, by the look of your chops.'

'What's dat?' asked Sal, pointing at the one-legged frog that was kicking in my hand.

'Nothing to do with you,' I said.

'I want it,' she said.

'Well, bad luck. I've only just found it.'

She tried to grab it but it was out of reach. When she screamed in the tin-roofed room, it was like having a tooth drilled. After that, it took her about twenty seconds to get undressed and climb in with me and Dad, and another five seconds for Sniff to work out where we were.

He'd been through the sticky-buds again, chasing something, and suddenly there he was with his great paws on the side of the bath, getting batted over the head by Sal with a plastic tugboat.

Normally, it's just impossible to get Sniff into a bath. That day, we found out how you do it. You put three people into the bath first and then you get the smallest, noisiest one to bat him over the head with a plastic tugboat and say 'Here, boy.' That's not quite enough to do the trick. The other two people in the bath have to scream: 'Get out! Don't you dare! Yuck, he's covered in sticky-buds! Get him off! Sniff, get off! Leave him, Sally! Don't wave that about . . .' and stuff like that. Ten seconds of that and he was so worked up, nothing would have kept him out. He backed up through the door of the outhouse, and for a split second it looked as though he had retreated but no — he was just taking a bit of a run at it.

Talk about eureka! Maybe that's really how Archimedes found out about displacement and all that. He was just lying in his tin tub having a peaceful soak, maybe trying out a new toy galley or something, and along comes this hound all covered in sticky-buds and dives in with him. When he yells *Eureka!*, he probably doesn't mean *I have found it*. What he probably means is, *Now look what you've done!*

It was dead lucky for those martins that they'd had the good sense to build up close to the roof, because any lower and their nifty little mud huts would have been washed away. We all jumped up, half-drowned and gasping for breath. Dad whipped Sal up in the air to save her from the tidal wave, and with a great *sloosh*, most of the bathwater went over the side.

So there we were, standing there starkers, with about a cupful of water left in the bath, having a good go at Sniff for leaving us all high and dry. And who was standing in the doorway with their eyes popping out, laughing their heads off? Tatty and Minta!

What could I do? Blushing like mad, I turned round and snatched at the nearest thing I could find to cover myself up — my shirt which I'd hung on one of the coat hooks. As soon as I'd grabbed hold of it, I remembered the harvest mouse I'd tucked in the pocket. By then, in that split second, I saw the poor little guy fly up in the air. I couldn't risk letting him hurt himself, so I had to cover up with one hand and dive backwards to catch the mouse with the other. Dad, Sal and Sniff all broke my fall but I finished up on my back in the bottom of the bath with a lump on the back of my head where I'd thumped it on the way down, and a nasty bruise on my backside where I'd sat on the tugboat.

Mum and Lolly had arrived by now and were trying to make sense of the scene which faced them.

'Hello, dear,' said Dad. He didn't seem to know quite what to do. He put Sal down and held Sniff in front of him. The prickly sticky-buds made him wince, but I don't suppose anyone else noticed because they were looking at me.

Tatty and Minta started rattling away.

'Oh no.'

'Poor *thing*!'

I could hardly believe it, but the twins had realized what a hero I was and they wanted to give me first aid. I groaned a bit and closed my eyes. My right hand was still holding the mouse out of harm's way and my left was keeping the wet shirt in place. I tried to arrange my face so that it read: *I am in agony but I can take it . . .*

'That's cruel, that is!'

Tatty grabbed my wrist and Minta prised the mouse out of my fist. Never mind that I'd nearly killed myself saving it from a nasty fall, the only thing they were worried about was the flipping animal!

'Has that boy squashed it or anything?'

'No, looks all right.'

'Lucky for him. Otherwise he'd have got a good thumping.'

They huffed off through the outhouse, taking with them the mouse I'd thought would send them into screams of panic. Sal was so keen to get out and see where they were going with the mouse that she used my head as a step.

Mum picked her up. 'I wish you'd said you were going to

bath Sal and Sniff, Rob,' she said. 'I'd have got her to bring a few more towels. And Ben dear, I shouldn't lie there for too long — I think you're putting off the martins. Those poor little babies must be starving.'

'Nice job you guys did on the pathways and stuff,' said Lolly.

'Oh, yes, lovely,' Mum agreed.

'Thanks,' Dad and I said, and off she went with Sal and Lolly.

'It's encouragement like that that makes it all worthwhile,' Dad said. He put Sniff down. Now that we had a bit of privacy, he didn't need to use him as a screen. The screen shook himself, spraying the whole place with a mixture of bathwater and sticky-buds, before trotting off outside.

'Did you hear what Tatty and Minta said, Dad? They threatened me. And their mum let them get away with it.'

'They are a bit formidable, aren't they, old son? That's because of all the aggro they've had at home from the mad poet,' he said.

'Yeah, and barging in here like that when we've got nothing on.'

'Ah,' he said, 'but I s'pose arty people don't get so uptight about having an audience when they're in the bath.'

'Yeah, well, that's the last one I'm having while they're staying next door,' I said. 'They've probably given me a complex or something.'

'Nice try,' said Dad. 'But I seem to remember that your fear of soap goes back way before Tatty and Minta appeared on the scene. Now cheer up, old lad,' he went on. 'We've got an afternoon at the seaside to look forward to.'

Seven

No way would Sniff get in the car that afternoon.

I thought it was obvious that the twins were upsetting him but I didn't say anything. Dad had one more go at getting him into the back. It was no good. This time, when he held up the tailgate door and whistled, Sniff zipped out from behind the cottages, galloped about ten metres towards the car, changed his mind, put his back brakes on, swerved sideways, bounced on his front elbows and buzzed off again.

'He's not interested,' called Mum from the front. 'Just leave him, Rob. He can't do any harm. He'll just settle down when we've gone and have a zizzo in the shade. There's food and water outside the back door for him if he wants it.'

'Stupid,' said Tatty, who was sitting with her legs crossed in Sniff's usual spot behind the back seat.

'Blinking nutter,' agreed Minta.

With you two sitting there, you'd have to be a blinking nutter to get in, I thought, but my lips were sealed. Mum would have killed me if I'd opened them. It was her idea to take Lolly and the twins to the coast in the first place. What with their motorbike needing a tune-up and all that, and with us having plenty of room in the Passat, she'd said, it would be a waste of a lovely sunny day for them not to come swimming.

'What do you say, girls?' she said. 'You wouldn't mind roughing it a bit and going in the boot with the dog, would you?'

The girls had moaned and mumbled about it, complaining that Sniff dribbled and his breath smelt and he was still damp and sticky-buddy and a real drag, so Mum had said, 'OK, why don't you two squeeze up on the back seat with Sal and your mum and Ben can get in the boot?'

'Why should *he* get all the leg-room?' Tatty moaned.

'Yeah!' said Minta. 'Why should we have to suffer and be all crunched up? We'll go in the boot.'

'Yeah!' said Tatty. 'And the dog can stay right down the far end and not come stinking us out.'

So now there I was, jammed between Sal and Lolly, not even next to a window, and feeling well cheesed off, and there was Dad, standing by the tailgate, whistling and calling, working himself up into a right wiggy. 'Come on, Sniff! Will you get in here!'

'Forget about it, love,' said Mum. 'He'll be all right. Let's go.'

'Why don't I stay and look after him?' I suggested. Mum gave me a look and a shake of the head. I'd already had a long lecture before lunch about being more considerate to people who were emotionally disturbed, so I shut up, folded my arms and suffered in silence. There I was, baking hot, doomed to spend an afternoon on a stupid beach with this bunch of creeps.

Dad slammed the tailgate, got in and started the car. No sign of the Sniffer. Off we went, bouncing up the track towards the lane.

All the windows were open, so the noise of the wind drowned out some of the dozy things that Tatty and Minta were rabbiting on about — although I couldn't help hearing one or two remarks.

'Could have drowned it.'

'Good thing we like got it off him.'

'What was he going to do with it?'

'Something stupid.'

'That's it, something stupid.'

'What did he want to like go and snatch it from the wild for?'

'Idiot.'

'Some owl or fox could have like starved to death with that mouse missing from the food chain.'

'Selfish.'

'He wants to watch it.'

I decided to rise above it and not answer back. I didn't say anything about Sal pounding me on my bump with her plastic spade, either. I just sat there, suffering and thinking of tortures, lovely tortures that would teach those horrible twins to respect me and understand what an ace person I really was. When we got to the beach, I would dig a huge hole, so deep that they couldn't climb up the sides, and lure them into it. Then I would drop crabs and seaweed and slithery eels on them. Or maybe I'd dig a channel that would let in cold seawater bit by bit until they begged for mercy. Then I might force them to eat jellyfish sandwiches or pour lugworms down the backs of their swimsuits.

The cool country lanes with the overhanging trees were like green tunnels. Some were so narrow that, by leaning across Sal, I could put my hand out of the window and get it slapped by the cow parsley growing on the bank. I hoped that Tatty and Minta were getting jealous because they couldn't get their arms out. They were.

'You want to watch it, Ben.'

'You can like break your arm doing that.'

Dad let it go for a while. We weren't going fast and he doesn't believe in being a spoilsport, so for a second or two I had some real fun testing my reflexes against the tickly weeds — and winding the twins up at the same time. It was all going great until Sal tried to climb out of her safety chair so that *she* could stick her arm out of the window and then Dad *had* to say something about it being dangerous and a bad idea. So back to boredom and smug giggles from behind me.

By now, we were out of the deep lanes, and as we turned the corner I suddenly caught sight of this really amazing thing. I could tell that I wasn't the only one to notice it because Tatty and Minta had stopped rabbiting and were kneeling up in the back with their noses pressed against the window. Imagine a giant slowly pulling a magnet under a ginormous sheet of paper with iron filings spread all over the top of it — it was a bit like that. Or maybe a bit like a submarine periscope that just cuts the surface of the water so that it looks split from underneath. Something was drawing a dark straight line through the middle of a solid yellow field of wheat and it was coming straight towards us!

I banged on the front seat and shouted, 'Stop the car, Dad!'

'What's the matter?' Dad slammed on the brakes.

'There! It's Sniff! He's following us!'

We all piled out to watch him do the last four hundred metres. With the engine turned off, you could hear him skittering like a speedboat, and as the line changed direction slightly, six or eight partridges went up like fireworks and made us all jump. And then he came bursting out of the wheat, puffing like a steam train and jumping from one person to the next until he got to Sal. When he'd given her a really good lick and knocked her over and made her laugh, he did a couple of backward rolls, then scrambled to his feet and took a running jump through the open tailgate into the boot, where he lay panting, thumping his tail and waving his tongue.

'He comin' wiv us,' Sal said.

'Well, he certainly does seem to have changed his mind!' said Mum.

'That really is amazing,' said Lolly. 'How on earth did he know which direction to take?'

'Just naturally brilliant,' I said, for the benefit of Fatty and Squinter.

'He knows the sound of the engine,' said Dad. 'With no other traffic on the roads, he can probably hear it for miles. Can't you, you pest?'

'*Rrralph!*' said Sniff.

The twins now decided that they weren't going back into the boot because they didn't want to get panted and dribbled on. Even Lolly thought they were being boringly wet, but to keep the peace, she agreed to get in the boot with me and to let the twins sit in the back with Sal.

As we set off again and Sniff went round and round over my feet and Lolly's while he banged his nose on the side windows and then on the back, I gave Lolly a little smile that meant: *Pity about your children being so immature. I am a more adult-type person and I don't mind sacrificing my comfort for a dumb animal.* As it happened, I was also thinking of the Everton mint humbug I had slipped into Sal's mouth before we got back into the car. It was my last one, and I really like Everton mints, especially chewy jumbo-sized ones, so normally I would have kept it and enjoyed a private suck later on in the afternoon. But giving it to Sal was a stroke of pure genius. It meant that, even if the twins managed to avoid getting whacked on the head by Sal's spade — which I doubted — they were certainly going to get *well* slimed.

We can't have been going for more than about two minutes before I heard the first *errrr!* as sticky spit ran down Sal's arm to her elbow and dripped on to Minta's leg.

Panic stations! Where were the Wet Wipes? Quick! There was a mass of urk everywhere and — *YUCK!* — Sal was trying to cuddle Tatty! Were they in the glove compartment? No.

'Sal,' pleaded Mum, 'let go of Minta! No, don't cry. I know you want to show her you love her. I *know* you do. But just let go and . . . Now you're dribbling, sweetheart. You're dribbling all over the place. What *have* you got in your mouth? Don't take it out! No, don't! Oh, now look! All down Minta's T-shirt! Oh, can't anybody find those Wet Wipes? This is hopeless . . .'

I knew it was hopeless, because a rather sharp pain in a place where I had recently collided with a plastic tugboat reminded me that I just happened to be sitting on the missing carton of Wet Wipes.

Yesterday the calamine lotion, today the Wet Wipes. Every little bump in the road was agony, but revenge was worth suffering for.

Eight

It was great at the beach. It turned out that there wasn't any sand, only pebbles, so there was no chance of digging elephant traps for the twins. But it didn't matter, because once they'd unstickied themselves by having a swim in the sea, they buzzed off by themselves somewhere and didn't bother me.

Mum, Dad and Lolly covered themselves in sun-tan oil and formed a sort of human playpen round Sal, who wouldn't wear any clothes. Now and then they chased wasps off her with rolled-up newspapers. It had been a waste of time cleaning her up since she spent the rest of the afternoon happily spreading ice cream all over her chubby self.

Sniff and I woofed our way through our 99s with extra sprinkle-spronkle, nuts and raspberry sauce, and then went down to the water to muck about. I skimmed some flat stones across the waves and he kept bouncing in after them and paddling madly back, yapping for more. When my arm started to ache and I stopped for a rest, he turned to meet the waves and snapped at the froth as they broke over him.

'That your dog?' a voice behind me asked.

I turned and saw a skinny kid wearing pink Bermuda shorts and yellow plastic sand shoes. He was about my age, with a long, serious face. His ears stuck out and were red and peeling on top. So were his shoulders. He saw me looking at them and peeled off a long strip of skin to show that it didn't bother him.

'We've been here a week,' he said, before I had a chance to reply. 'What kind of dog is that?'

'Bit of everything,' I said. 'Bit of sheepdog, probably. See the way he tries to round up the waves?'

'Oh, yeah,' said the peeling kid, his serious face looking even more serious when he was impressed. 'Does he fetch?'

'Try him,' I said, and the kid chucked a couple of pebbles over Sniff's head into the sea. For a skinny kid, he was an excellent thrower. He didn't waste any effort winding up, just pulled back and snapped from the hip.

Every time he chucked something, Sniff shot out of the water, came down in it with a massive great splash and then bobbed up again, looking hopeful. The kid laughed. 'Good, isn't he? Good swimmer. What's his name?'

I told him.

'Would you like to see something interesting?' he said.

'What?'

'Come on, I'll show you.' He ran along the water's edge, splashing and crunching. I walked fast after him, wishing I had something on my feet but trying to look as though I didn't care. I followed him round the corner beyond the concrete slab that Dad had explained was probably an emplacement for an anti-aircraft gun during the war.

'D'you mean that?' I asked, pointing at the slab. 'Is that the interesting thing?'

'No,' he said, and ran on.

'That's a gun emplacement,' I said, but he just nodded as if he knew already, and kept going.

There were hardly any people on this part of the beach, only two lovers cuddling under the cliffs. The beach and the cliff stretched away for miles into the distance, right along to Sheringham or Cromer — I wasn't sure which it was. Sniff lost interest in the waves and went off to have a look at the lovers. I think he might have touched the lady's leg with his cold nose, because she suddenly screamed and sat up.

'Whoo! I say! Kissy-kissy!' yelled the peeling kid. Then he shouted, 'Come on, Sniff!' as though he was talking to his own dog. Sniff started to come, stopped, changed his mind, had a good look at a pile of clothes, peed on one of the bloke's shoes, grabbed the other in his teeth and ran off along the base of the cliff.

'Oy!' screamed the bloke, jumping up and lobbing grenade-sized lumps of earth after him. When he saw he had no chance of landing one anywhere near Sniff, he altered his aim and started bombarding me and the kid. We legged it out of range as quickly as we could.

'I wish you'd stop shouting his name about!' I panted to the kid. 'That bloke'll be able to trace us now. That's if he doesn't murder us when we go back again.'

'Don't worry,' he puffed. 'Hopeless shot. Poor arm action, did you notice? Anyway, we'll go back along the top. We can get up the cliff further along, no problem. See where it's slid down?' He pointed to a spot about a kilometre ahead.

Didn't look to easy to me, but I didn't say so.

Once we were well out of range of the lover bloke's bombardment, the kid stopped running along in the shallow water and started to move sideways up the beach. 'Here,' he called over his shoulder. 'This is what I was going to show you.' He stopped, licked his finger and held it up, then he closed one eye and waited a sec before he was satisfied. 'We're OK,' he went on. 'We're downwind of it.'

I limped over to where he was squatting. My feet were sore now.

'Well? What d'you think?'

From on top of the cliff, you would have thought it was just a big old sack of something. It lay among the seaweed on the tideline where the buzz of flies was loud enough to be heard above the crashing of the waves and the grating noise of the pebbles as the sea rolled back. There wasn't a mark on it. It was smooth and solid-looking, except at the curve of the neck, where the fur was ruffled. Its head was tucked almost under its body, but you could see one big staring eye and two rows of grinning teeth.

'Wow,' I said. Sniff came up, dropped the shoe, and tucked himself under my arm where I was squatting. He stayed by me, panting quietly — respectfully, you could say. It was a beautiful thing, the seal, even though it was dead.

'It's probably come from Blakeney Point,' the kid said. He sounded as if he was talking in church. 'There's a big colony there.'

'We should tell somebody,' I said.

'Why?' he said.

'Well, in case it's got . . . you know . . . the seal virus.'

57

'Gosh!' he said. 'You're right. I didn't think of that — but I knew you'd be interested, didn't I?'

He straightened up. 'Come on, we'd better get on to the RSPCA straight away. There's a phone back in the car park. This way!' That was one thing I noticed about this kid: he just made up his mind about things and then did them.

His plastic shoes sprayed pebbles. Sniff bounced after him, woofing with excitement, and I hobbled after the pair of them. First, we had to go in the opposite direction from the car park, towards the place where the cliff had collapsed and loose red earth was piled into a curving slope. It was even steeper than it looked from a distance and there was one section near the top that was almost vertical. OK, you could make out a zig-zag trail where other people had been up before, but it still looked tough.

It was one of the scariest things I've ever done in my life, climbing up there, especially as Sniff just dashed about on titchy little ledges without realizing that one slip meant he would drop about a zillion metres on to the pebbles. Getting him up the vertical section took some doing, but the kid went up ahead and pulled while I pushed. When we came to the trickiest bit of all, where there was no way Sniff could go on without us actually lifting him, he did start to look a bit worried, but the kid talked to him and tickled him in his favorite spot, just behind the ear, and that seemed to give him his confidence back. After that, it was just a question of taking it slow and steady and not making any mistakes.

In about three minutes, we were at the top, lying flat on the grassy path, catching our breath and grinning like real heroes. Not far away, beyond some newly ploughed fields and across the flat salt marshes, you could see a white windmill. It felt as if we were the first people in the world ever to see it.

Once we'd got our breath back, we started jogging in the direction of the car park and the crowded part of the beach — and I thought how great it was to have grass under your bare feet rather than pebbles. We stopped once — to check whether the lovers were still around. They were too busy kissing to notice us. I could see the kid was going to call down 'kissy-kissy' again, so I put my hand over his mouth and dragged him away from the edge of the cliff, both of us giggling like loonies. Sniff went 'Rrraalph!' and I had to drag *him* away by the scruff, too. Even so, we couldn't resist chucking a couple of handfuls of weeds on top of them, just to wind them up, before we all bunked it along the cliff path. The kid panted to me that *never*, no *way*, would you ever catch him wasting a nice day lying around *snogging* like that. I told him me neither.

The wind was getting up quite strongly by the time we got to the phone box. It was one of those old-fashioned red ones with such a stiff door that you wonder if it's actually a door at all, because opening it is like trying to rip one of the walls off. Anyway, after a struggle, we managed to get into it — not Sniff, because he doesn't like being shut in — and it was nice to see that it had a fairly up-to-date directory. Outside, there was a bunch of sailing dinghies lined up on their trailers, their wires zinging away against their aluminium masts and their pennants snapping.

Maybe that's why we didn't notice the man tapping on the glass.

We looked under RSPCA and it said to look under Royal Society for the Prevention of Cruelty to Animals, so we did. It was so hot in that box, especially after our run, that our fingers left wet marks on the pages. We found the number and dialled. Then the kid took the phone, because he'd supplied the 10p. We hung on for a long time and the box began to get steamy. The kid's ears and shoulders went the colour of beetroot. He pulled off a couple more strips of skin. Finally, someone answered.

'Hello, RSPCA? Ah. Well, I want to report a dead seal. Pardon?' He could see I was dying to hear what was going on so he held the receiver out.

Tap tap tap. Boy, that wind was getting strong. I put my ear as close to the phone as I could and concentrated on the thin voice.

Where exactly was this animal?

The kid explained pretty well.

Was there any sign of damage?

'No. Not really.'

Was there a bloody discharge from its nasal passages? The kid looked at me. I shook my head.

Tap tap tap tap!

'No.'

Did it look skinny or starved?

'Well, no. Quite sort of hefty, actually. . .eh?' I nodded in agreement.

How big was it?

'Metre and a half,' I said, and the kid passed it on.

Fairly typical for an adult common seal. Was it greyish brown?

60

'A bit sort of blotchy, I'd say,' said the kid.

Mottled? asked the man. *Yes, that'll be a common seal. And from what you say, it's died of natural causes. I take it you're ringing because you're worried it might have phocine distemper virus?*'

'Uh-huh,' we both said. The virus bit sounded right, anyway.

Well, I doubt that you need worry. And I'm happy to tell you that the epidemic seems to be over, except in one or two isolated areas off the coast of Scotland. Still, it's always best to be on the safe side, and we'll send someone down to check as soon as possible. Very kind of you to pass on the information, Mr . . . er?

'Spalderton,' said the kid. 'Edward Spalderton.'

Tap tap tap tap!

I thought 'Spalderton?' — but I didn't have time to focus on it because something important occurred to me.

'Ask him if it's dangerous to dogs, this distemper virus,' I said, remembering we'd had to get Sniff inoculated against distemper. I heard the bloke say that there was no evidence that the virus affected dogs at all and —

WHAM! Just like that, the door was whipped open, and a hand the size of a bunch of bananas grabbed Edward by the shoulder. He was ripped out of the phone booth as easily as pulling a tissue out of a box. Before I could say a word, the hand came back for me and I was yanked out too and sent spinning on to the gravel. It hurt.

Nine

He was one of the hairiest blokes I've ever seen. There were horrible black tufts sprouting out of his face, his ears, his nose, under his dirty vest — everywhere except the top of his head, which was as bald and pale as a hard-boiled egg. Even the finger he was pointing threateningly at me and Edward was thick with hair at the knuckles. He had a monster ring on every finger — skulls and eyes mostly — and apart from his grey vest, he was wearing a motorbiker's leather trousers and zip-up boots. Very 'heavy metal'.

'I don't like being kept waiting!' he barked. 'I don't like being mucked about when I've got an important call to make. You're lucky you never got this round your lughole!' He showed us a fistful of rings.

Suddenly, Sniff came zooming out from under a nearby Range Rover, where he'd been keeping his head down.

When people hold their arms out, it always has the same weird effect on him, and he took a running jump, banged his head on the underside of the bloke's arm, did a somersault and fell on his back. He did it again about ten times, making a hysterical yiking noise. The people passing must have thought the bloke was the type who gets his kicks by bouncing dumb animals like beach balls. A woman with a toy poodle tucked under one arm and a beach umbrella under the other started yapping at the bloke to leave the poor doggy alone, not realizing that the bloke was frozen by shock into a Statue of Liberty position. Sniff was going up and down like a pat-a-ball on a piece of elastic, so she hoiked her umbrella up like Sir Lancelot, and jabbed Mr Hairy right in the middle of the back.

Meanwhile, Edward, who had shot off at amazing speed as soon as the bloke had let go of him, was already out of sight. Once the lady's husband turned up and the argument with Mr Hairy really got going, I was off too, staggering over the rough ground in the direction I thought Edward had taken, and wishing I was wearing trainers.

By the time I'd got to the top of the steps past the ice-cream stall, Sniff had caught up with me and I was glancing over my shoulder to see if there was any sign of Mr Hairy — when I ran slap bang into Lolly and the twins. They were still wearing their beach gear and their arms were loaded with their other clothes — and they were in a tearing hurry. There was panic in their faces. They didn't stop to explain anything, just pushed past me like people out of a disaster movie. Right behind them came Mum, with a load of picnic stuff and more clothes — some of them mine. Dad, with Sal on his shoulders, was behind Mum, and Sniff practically knocked him down the steps by jumping up to lick Sal's bare toes.

Mum caught me by the arm. Something told me things weren't too cool on the beach.

'Where've you been?' said Dad. 'I've been searching all over the place for you? Why can't you ever say something before you disappear off the face of the earth?'

We were heading for the dirt track that wound into the salt marsh, where our car was parked. Dad didn't like using car parks if he could help it.

'What's happened?' I asked. 'Why are we leaving?'

Nobody wanted to waste time explaining and it wasn't until we were halfway back to the cottage that I could piece the story together from the scraps of information I got.

Tatty and Minta had apparently gone to the village store to buy some pop magazines. They were just leaving when they saw their dad coming out of the pub opposite. He didn't see them and they ducked back inside the shop till he disappeared round the corner. They were just making a run for it when they heard someone shouting. Their dad had spotted them, and was coming after them. They threw him off the scent by turning down the track that led to the windmill and then doubling back through the car park to the beach. That gave them just enough time to warn Lolly and to get everyone into the car and away.

Oh, crikey! I thought. That must have been him! Mr Hairy was Tatty and Minta's dad!

Before I could say anything, Dad said to the twins, 'You don't think there's any way he could have followed you down to the beach and seen you talking to us?' He flicked his eyes up to the rear-view mirror to catch their reaction. We'd left the coast road now and were heading inland.

'No way,' they said.

'And what was he driving?' Dad wanted to know.

'He was on foot when he saw us,' Tatty told him.

'I know that. But what did he drive to the beach? How did he get to Norfolk in the first place? What kind of car?'

'George doesn't drive a car,' Lolly explained. 'He rides a bike, a Norton.'

'A motorbike?' Mum asked.

'Oh, *Mum!*' I said.

'OK, OK!' she said. 'Pardon my ignorance.'

Something suddenly clicked. 'I saw it!' I yelled. 'Silver grey strip with red trim, with twin exhausts and peardrop silencers?'

'That's it,' said Lolly, looking sick.

'It was parked just behind the fruit stall on the prom, near the top of those steps that go down to the beach. Didn't you see it?'

Nobody else had.

Suddenly everyone was looking out of the back window with the same thing in mind. But there was no sign of any motorbike ripping after us.

'Right, then,' Dad said. 'If he didn't see any of us and he didn't see the car, I think we can safely assume that he won't be able to trace you. You can enjoy the rest of your holiday in peace.'

Lolly was thoughtfully running her finger over her black eye, so I thought maybe this was not the moment to mention the fact that I'd had the pleasure of meeting her nice, sweet-tempered husband in a phone box.

My mind began to race. Why was he in such a hurry to use the phone? Did he have an accomplice at another beach along the coast? Had he seen Lolly with Mum and Dad and

Sal on the beach? Did he realize that Sniff and I were with them? Did he follow Sniff back to the beach? What if he'd seen us all legging it towards the getaway car! Oh, no! Without realizing it, I could easily have put him right on our trail!

But if that was the case, how come he wasn't following us now? I took another nervous look out of the tailgate window. All clear. Phew!

'So what *did* happen to you?' It was Mum who broke my train of thought. 'Where did you get to?'

That was when I suddenly remembered Edward!

I started to explain about meeting this skinny, serious kid, finding the seal and climbing the cliff and everything. I had to work out in my head at the same time how I was going to steer round the bit about getting dragged out of the phone box by George. No point in getting anybody more scared than they were already.

And what a bummer not to have been able to exchange addresses with Edward, not to have said goodbye, even. I really liked him — he was a laugh. Now I'd probably never see him again.

On the other hand, if we were going to get worked over by some heavy metal poet with a grudge, he was well out of it.

Ten

Tea was a pretty mizz bizz, even though there were nice thick chunks of real white bread (luckily, that was all they had at the corner shop in Spalderton village), real butter (supplied by Lolly, who didn't seem to have heard of polyunsaturated fats), hazelnut spread, and some luscious fudge brownies out of a packet.

Lolly and the twins just played with their food, picking the fudge off their brownies and flicking it at Sniff in a naffed off, limp sort of way. He was lying under the kitchen table with his head sticking out by Sal's chair, so that if the worst came to the worst and nobody saved him any scraps, he could at least lick a bit of hazelnut spread off her — hazelnut spread being her favourite and his. As it turned out, he must have thought it was his birthday, because grub that nobody in their right minds would normally save for him kept bombing over from the twins' side of the table. *Woomph! Woomph!* He looked as though he was attacking a swarm of flies.

Lolly was so down and the twins were such a drag that it was a relief when they finally wandered back to Number

Two to be miserable on their own. Mum and Dad kept saying what a shame it was and how demoralized they looked and everything. I thought they were the biggest bunch of pains ever, but I could see I'd only get a lecture if I said anything. I had this ugly feeling that Mum might suggest talking over their problem in a group situation, so I melted into the background and let her and Dad form their own group over the washing-up. I dived on to the squashy sofa next door and tried to make myself invisible.

Sal was gawping at some kiddie programme on the black and white clockwork TV, and I was caught between two of the worst kind of conversations you can imagine. On one side, Keith Chegwin and Mandy Tulloch were blahing away on the telly, and on the other, behind the kitchen door, Mum and Dad were getting into their favourite subject — other people's problems.

Mum was asking what Dad was going to do if Lolly's husband came looking for them. What if it came to a confrontation? George was a violent man, judging by Lolly's technicolour eye.

On the TV, Cheggers wanted to know what Mandy's sexiest colour fruit gum was.

Dad was trying to be cool about it. He would reason with the man. He would persuade him to return home and — er — consult a marriage guidance counsellor or something.

Some hope, I thought. That bloke needs a keeper, not a counsellor.

Mandy Tulloch was asking everyone to write in with their vote on the sexiest colour socks Cheggers had ever worn.

'Anyway, I keep telling you not to worry about him,' Dad

went on. 'We're miles from anywhere here. He's never going to find this place.'

'But if he does find it, we can't phone, we can't get help . . .'

'I told you, I'll handle him,' said Dad.

I thought about the row of rings on that great hairy fist. Dad was no wimp, but that bloke could do some damage.

'And what if he gets past us? Sneaks into Number Two before we see him? What are we going to do then?' asked Mum.

'We'll just have to make sure he doesn't,' Dad told her.

'How?'

'I'm working on it,' said Dad, but he didn't sound all that convincing.

I thought maybe I'd better get working on it, too. Quietly, so as not to unglue Sal's attention from the telly, I opened the front door and slipped outside. Sniff was right behind me. He couldn't care less what colour socks Cheggers wore either.

The first thing I did was head for the greengage tree. I was soon up at lookout height and thinking to myself that maybe this was the answer. All we had to do was mount a twenty-four-hour watch up here, because you got a great view of the track through the barley field . . .

But who was going to go on watch? None of the grown-ups were going to fancy climbing up here, and even if the twins *could*, I doubted if they would. So that was a dead loss.

The sound of Sniff skittering about below made me look down. There was a whirring of wings, and a pheasant clattered out of harm's way by flying low over the boundary hedge by Number Two's outside loo. It turned and banked to the right, making its dry *cough-cough-cough* noise, soaring over the tangle of trees and bushes in the far corner. The late afternoon sun made the reds and greens on the bird's neck flash like neon lights, just as it skimmed the peeling white roof of the almost-hidden caravan.

The caravan! Why hadn't I thought of that before? That was the answer! The only problem was — how to make a pathway to it that wouldn't give it away. If I could work that one out, it would make an ace hideout!

I let myself down from the lookout tree a touch more carefully than the last time, and dropped on to all fours among the crunchy cut nettles, with no damage done to skin or jeans. I followed the scythed path round to the back of Number Two and then headed for the outside loo.

A voice nearly made me jump out of my skin.

'Use your own!' It was Tatty or Minta. They were standing by their back door, making threatening signs in my direction.

'Yeah, bog off!' That was definitely Minta. She thought she was well funny. 'Get it?' she went on, really chuffed with her joke. 'Keep off our bog, stay on your own.'

'Don't be daft,' I said. 'I'm not going in there.'

'Well, what *are* you doing?' they asked, as they closed the back door and put on their leather jackets, even though it was still dead warm out. I figured that they were going to cheer themselves up by giving me a good thumping. If they were trying to look hard in their leather gear, they weren't doing a bad job.

I decided that the best form of defence was attack. 'Why don't you come and find out?' I said.

'Fancies itself,' said Tatty, advancing.

'Does, doesn't it?' agreed Minta, screwing up her eyes as she slipped her wire-framed gogs into her pocket and got into step with her twin sister. Blimey, they meant business.

'Wait there,' I said, holding up my hand, and I moved so fast I left them standing. They had to content themselves with mickey-taking noises while I sprinted round the side of our cottage and in through the front door.

I was out again inside thirty seconds and round the back of the house in another shake.

'We thought you'd gone to tell your daddy,' sneered Tatty.

'Or to find a big stick,' Minta joined in. I noticed she'd put her gogs back on.

'I went to find these,' I said, and held out the contents of the coronation tea caddy — four different keys. 'Found these this morning,' I went on, since, although not exactly enthusiastic, they were at least looking, and not saying anything nasty. 'And I reckon one of them might open up that old caravan. I thought you might like to come with me and find out.'

'What caravan?' said Tatty, suspicious, but a weeny bit more interested.

'I'll show you,' I said. I jumped to catch the lowest branch of the lookout tree and pulled myself up. 'Can you climb?' I wheezed.

'Why? Got the caravan up there, have you?' said Tatty with a cackle, and whacked Minta's leather shoulder to make

71

sure she appreciated a joke that was as good as the one about bogs.

'No, but you can see it from here.'

They were good climbers, I'll say that. Neither of them needed a leg up. They just took a run and swung themselves up and over the lowest branch, and then they were away, swarming up to lookout level, no trouble at all. It was like being on a ship in a storm to be up the top of that old tree with those two shaking it about.

You could tell they thought it was good up there, because as soon as they reached the level where you could see right over the roof to Spalderton Hall, with the sun even redder on the windows than when I'd first seen it, they stopped wisecracking and just enjoyed the view.

'Try one of these,' I said, and threw them each a greengage.

'What's this?' said Tatty.

'It's a greengage. Try it.'

'Yuck! It's not ripe, it's still like green,' said Minta, and pulled back her arm to buzz hers away.

'Just bite it,' I said. 'You can spit it out if you don't like it.'

Very carefully, suspecting a trap but not wanting to chicken out, they bit through the skin. It wasn't long before they were both chewing away like crazy, and looking around for more.

There were just half a dozen left, right up at the very top and within my reach. We polished them off, relishing every mouthful.

'Seen it?' I asked, when the last of the greengage stones had been sucked clean and spat out.

'Seen what?' said Tatty.

'The caravan.'

'There *is* one, is there?' said Minta. 'You're not just mucking about?'

'No, no kidding,' I said. 'There, look.'

'Oh, yeah! I see it now!'

'That's amazing,' said Minta. 'There's no way you can like see it from the cottage, not with all that stuff growing round it. And it looks quite big from here.'

'I was thinking,' I said, 'that if I . . . we . . . could somehow get to it without giving away that it was there. . .'

'. . . it would be a great little spot to hide out!' Tatty said.

'What are we waiting for?' said Minta and swung down.

Tatty and I dropped down beside her and we all had a good look at the situation from ground level.

One obvious route was to follow the boundary hedge at the back of Number One's garden right along behind both the brick lavs. The problem, though, was not just the ginormous nettles but, even worse, the tangle of huge great prickly shrubs and things.

'Don't fancy trying to get through that way,' I said. 'Look at that.' Some of the brambles that were sprouting up into the hawthorn hedge must have been two or three metres long.

'Painful,' said Minta. 'And those goosegog bushes could do you a mischief, too. Look at the spikes on them! But — hey! — nice goosegogs, look. Big yellow juicy ones. I bet they're sweet.'

'You can go in and get them,' I said. '*I'm* not.'

'And there's raspberries. Those are raspberry canes, all

73

overgrown!' said Tatty. 'Hey, what a drag we can't get to them! I should think this must have been a thingy, a — not a nursery. What do I mean, Minta?'

'A kitchen garden?' said Minta.

'That's it, yeah.'

'No way I fancy tunnelling through that lot,' I said. 'You'd get scratched to death crawling through there. Tell you what, let's see if there's a way through from over there.' I pointed towards the far hedge on their side of the garden.

'What d'you reckon, Minta?' said Tatty, not wanting to be the one to say OK.

'What d'you reckon?' Minta said back.

'Well, maybe,' said Tatty.

'My man!' I said. 'Gimmee five!'

'I don't believe this kid! He is *so* uncool!' said Tatty, but she let her hand be slapped anyway, and so did Minta.

'Let's go!' I said.

'Listen, Tarzan,' said Minta. 'You're not the only one who does the "let's go" bit — right?'

'OK! OK!' I said.

'So, let's go,' she said. And we went.

When we looked back towards Number Two from the top corner of their garden, there was Lolly's motorbike and sidecar, sort of leaning against each other in the newly cut driveway round the side of Number One. It made you think of a couple of animals quietly chewing the cud on a hot afternoon.

'Wish we could get that hidden somewhere,' said Tatty. 'That's a dead giveaway, that is, if George does turn up and start nosing around.' They always called him George, I noticed. It would have been too uncool to call him Dad.

'We could maybe stick it in the outhouse, next to the bathroom,' I suggested, 'if we took the old bikes out.'

'Hey, that's not a bad idea!' said Minta. 'Sometimes you're not as stupid as you look.'

'Thanks a bunch,' I said.

Tatty, meanwhile, was concentrating on the problem of the caravan. 'I s'pose you could crawl through there . . .' she said, almost to herself. She was poking a long stick into a gap between a sticky-bud bush and a rusty clump of ragwort. 'At least there aren't any stingers here.'

'No, thanks,' said Minta.

Sniff suddenly materialized with a big flint in his mouth. He dropped it, lay down beside it and did a *rrralphh* to show that he wanted someone to chuck it for him.

'Where'd he spring from?' asked Tatty, as Sniff whined and pulled at the flint with his paws.

'Didn't see. Wasn't like looking,' said Minta.

I took a pretend run at his stone and Sniff grabbed it, spun round — and disappeared.

He'd dived into the undergrowth between the hawthorn hedge and the overgrown privet and laurel bushes that formed a screen in front of the caravan. There was a whole mass of tall grasses, ground elder and dock leaves growing together. If you squatted down, you could see a little trail, just a few centimetres wide. One way, it went towards the house and then turned off through a little gap in the boundary hedge. The other way, it went up the garden towards the corner and seemed to stop just where the dock leaves were thickest.

'Must be a rabbit run or something,' I said. 'What say we try following it through these dock leaves?'

'After you,' said Tatty and Minta, shaking their heads as if I was crazy.

At first it looked impossible because, once you'd crawled a couple of metres, you came to this bush with dry twigs, all tangled together, that twanged against your ears and scratched your face.

The good thing was, though, that they were old and brittle and easy to snap. So in a couple of minutes, by breaking some dry twigs off and tucking some of the greener, bendier ones out of the way, I'd made a kind of cave in the undergrowth. I crawled forward and found I could almost sit up, and then, guided partly by Sniff's growling and panting, I gradually worked my way towards a place where the leaves crisscrossed so tightly that they made a thick sort of curtain.

I dug my hand through, pulled the curtain to one side — and suddenly, there it was.

Eleven

A notice on the door of the caravan read KEEP OUT OR YOU DYE.

'What do you think?' I said to Tatty and Minta, who had crawled through the last part of the rabbit run to join me in the clearing, just by the three little steps leading up to the caravan door.

'Cute, isn't it!' said Minta, hooking on her gogs to get a better look, and blinking in the semi-darkness.

'Hey, this is really cool,' said Tatty. 'It's a really diddy little thing!'

I could see what she meant. It was like one of those snowstorm things with a snowman or a Christmas tree inside a glass bubble — you shake the bubble and all the snow stuff goes swirling around in the water. Only here, the bubble was made of leaves and branches and the 'snow' was made by zillions of dancing points of light shining through the tangled leaves and twigs.

The caravan itself was tiny, with a curved roof. The two little windows on either side of the door had drawn purple curtains. It was white, peeling a bit in places, and it had a stovepipe chimney sticking out of the top. I guessed it was pretty old and that it had been there for ages. If it had ever had wheels, there was no sign of them now. Somebody had jacked it up and rested it on four brick pillars.

'Fancy trying the keys, either of you?' I asked.

'Scared of the gypsy's curse?' teased Tatty, indicating the notice on the door.

'No,' I said. 'I didn't want you moaning on about Tarzan going first all the time, that's all.' That wasn't quite true, because it's not that easy to put death threats out of your mind, even if the person who makes them isn't too hot on spelling.

'Oh, yeah?' said Minta.

'Look, hurry up, will you!' said Tatty. 'It'll be dark pretty soon. Stop fiddling about and get the door open. Let's have a look inside, for Pete's sake.'

Two of the keys looked as though they might fit in the lock. The first one went in — and wouldn't come out again.

'Here, let me have a go,' said Tatty, shoving me aside after I'd tugged at it for a while. 'You don't want brute force and ignorance for a job like this, you need. . .uh! There you go — it's out. Pass me that other one. And *do* keep your fat head out of the light! It's tricky enough as it is.'

There was something in her voice that told me I wasn't the only one who was nervous, so I didn't make a big deal out of it, and I pressed back as far as I could into the privet behind me. As I did so, I felt my head burst a spider's web. I brushed my hand over my hair and there was a tickle on the back of my hand as a fair-sized spider scuttled across it and up my arm. It was one of those fat ones with a cross shape on its back. I flicked it sideways without much thought. At that, Minta screamed so loud, you'd have thought it was a tarantula or a scorpion. Then just for a second — it can't have been more than that — she looked so embarrassed with herself for doing her nut over a spider that I even felt sorry for her.

'It's OK, it's OK!' I yelled, but the scream scared me rigid, and Tatty, who that very second had got the door unlocked, dived sideways as though she'd been electrocuted. The door creaked open slowly, gathered speed and then smacked back against the wall of the caravan.

We all kept still, our hearts pounding away, peering into the dark interior. It was spooky, making me think of booby traps, so I guessed that's what the others were thinking about, too. While we were all sitting there in the green gloom with our mouths open, hardly daring to breathe, there was a sudden crash in the undergrowth.

'Ahh!' we all went.

Sniff came slamming into us, wriggling and panting hot breath and slobbering over everybody. It was impossible in the cramped space to avoid getting a whacking either from his tail or his tongue.

'Geddim off!' groaned the twins.

'Thanks a bunch, boy,' I said, trying to get a grip on him. Judging by the barley stalk stuck behind his ear like a greengrocer's pencil, he'd been charging about in the field again.

As soon as he'd given us all a good going-over, he turned round, saw the open door, and hopped up the three steps and

79

into the caravan. Sniff wasn't the sort of dog who worried about 'Keep Out' notices.

We strained our ears and we could hear him bumping around inside, and things falling over, but nothing like the clang of steel jaws springing together or the whoosh of triggered poison darts. After about ten seconds, he appeared at the door again, trying to shake the life out of a plastic Star Wars light-sword.

'Oh, *well* scary!' said Tatty and Minta together, and we all bundled in.

It was wicked inside, a bit musty, but dry and quite clean. At one end, there was a little table that seemed to be hinged to the far wall. Along the shorter wall there was a long seat, which was probably a bunk as well, with built-in cupboards above it. There were a couple of camp stools (knocked over by Sniff) and not much else. To the right as you went in, there was a narrow sort of corridor that took you past a teeny kitchen area with a sink and draining board, and a little stove, plate racks and more cupboards. And then at the end was a bedroom space with bunk beds.

Sniff had decided to have a lie-down on the bottom bunk, and he was noisily chewing his light-sword. Pinned above the top bunk was a longish strip of computer printout: you could just about see the holes along the sides of it, but there wasn't enough light to see the words.

My foot dinked against something under the bottom bunk. I bent down and found a saucer with a stub of candle in it. I guessed that if there was a candle, there might well be some matches lying about too, and sure enough, a quick feel around the saucer and my hand knocked against a small box that rattled. I felt the twins breathing impatiently as I fumbled with the matches. The first ones I tried to strike were spent but the third one spluttered and caught.

I lit the candle, and there was the message, written in big capitals on a computer by someone without a spellcheck:

YOU ARE TREPASING. LEAVE NOW OR IT COULD BE FAITLE.

'It's only one of Germ's kids,' said Tatty. 'Probably Rory, he's the oldest.'

I thought of all the Dungeons and Dragons manuals and the posters in my room, and I remembered thinking when I first went in there that one shelf looked as though it had been set up for a computer. So that was Rory's room.

'Typical male chauvinist piggy attitude,' sneered Minta, the candle flame dancing in her round lenses.

'He just doesn't want anyone mucking about with his stuff. That's fair enough, isn't it?' I said.

'Trust you to stick up for him!' said Tatty.

'I'm just saying it's a bluff, that's all. He's trying to scare off anybody who might come sneaking around.' I almost convinced myself, anyway.

'Whatever,' said Minta. 'The important thing is — we've found the caravan. We've found a good way into it, and it could come in handy if we need like a really secure hiding place.'

'The only trouble is,' said Tatty, 'we wouldn't have enough warning to get out of our cottage and into here before George saw us.'

'I've been giving that a bit of thought,' I said. 'I've got this idea for improving security. Tell you what, tomorrow we'll clear out those old bikes, make room in the outhouse to put the motorbike and sidecar out of sight and have a crack at putting together a surveillance system. OK by you?'

'OK, why not?' the twins said.

'Right,' I said. 'So let's lock up and get out of here for now.'

'Can I like say something?' said Minta.

'Yeah, what?' I said.

'Well, just because you keep like coming up with these bright ideas, don't start thinking we're going to be in your gang or anything, OK? Because it's a real drag just following boys around. Right?'

'Right.'

'So give us the key and let's get out of here and lock up,' said Tatty. 'We're going.'

Boy, those two could be touchy.

Twelve

The sparrows bombing about in the ivy outside my little round window woke me. They really knew how to whirr and cheep. It took me a minute, staring at the V of the ceiling, before I worked out where I was. Then I let my eyes stray while I tried to remember what I was going to do today.

I noticed, without paying any real attention to it at first, that on top of the blue wardrobe, half-hidden behind a heap of paperback books, was an old portable TV set. While I was asking myself how I'd managed to miss it suddenly a whole bunch of things came into my head at the same time: my plan to improve security; a row of skull rings on a fist; a very hairy armpit; the juice of the last greengage; someone going *kissy-kissy*; the video camera that we'd packed into the side panel of the Passat, and the boxes of electric cable and stuff that Dad had brought to replace some of the dangerous old wiring in our cottage. I squinted at my watch . . . seven thirty-one. Right.

I went to the window to check the distance to the lookout tree. Eight metres, ten? Right. I heard voices from below, leaned out of the window and saw that the ground in front of the lean-to between the two cottages was littered with bikes. One of them was upside down on its saddle and handlebars. Tatty was kneeling by the free-spinning front wheel with an oil can in her hand, her ear to the hub of the wheel, listening. Minta was squatting nearby, fixing one of the other bikes. She was grunting with the effort of prising a link off the chain, using a screwdriver and a pair of snub-nosed pliers like somebody who'd used them before. A heap of mucky rags, the shine on the spokes and wheels, the dirt-free frames and the smooth, quiet race of the wheel on Tatty's bike showed that they'd been working for some time.

So they'd decided to work on some plan of their own, eh?

I got dressed in ten seconds flat and started collecting what I needed. I clambered on to the chest of drawers, carefully lifted down the TV — only another black and white job, an 'Elizabethan', but it would do if it worked. I plugged it in, switched it on, waved the aerial about a bit and — *fizz fizz, de-DAH!* — the test card. Great, we were in business. I switched it off and looked around. One bow . . . good, and a bamboo cane for an arrow . . . ace! I chucked them on to the bed. There had to be some string . . . yes, I thought Rory would be the type not to chuck good string away: plenty there. Now what? I still needed the coaxial extension lead, an extension lead for the mains supply, an A/C adaptor, the video camera and a nesting box. That one in the bathroom that the martins had turned their noses up at would do nicely. But first things first.

I unravelled the string, laying it out carefully on the floor so as not to get it tangled, and tied one end of it to the thick end of the bamboo cane. I elbowed the window wide open, fitted the bowstring behind the end of the 'arrow', aimed high over the trees and pulled, ducking my right shoulder quickly so as not to snag on the string that went snaking off out of the window. I hadn't tried for too much power and watched as the arrow dropped *just* over the greengage tree and dangled high up. That would be OK, I thought. Now for the next step.

The twins looked up sharply, saw me standing at the window, and the string trailing out, looped over the greengage tree. Then they decided to ignore me and started beavering away harder than ever.

There was no sign that Mum and Dad were about yet, and I thought it might not go down too well if I woke them up to tell what I had in mind. Sometimes it's better not to discuss your plans with your parents because they think about things for too long, and keep coming up with BUTs.

So I crept downstairs, stepping over Sniff, who was lying flat out on the landing. He opened one eye, and when I put my finger to my lips and went *shhhhh*, he pricked up his ears and pounded down the stairs like a madman. It's a waste of time trying to keep secrets from that dog.

I grabbed the car keys from the mantelpiece and let Sniff out of the front door before he woke everybody up — and I left him outside when I came back with the video camera, the adaptor, some masking tape, and the two extension leads I needed. I knew Dad had another couple in the house, so there was nothing to stop him pressing on with the rewiring. I left the camera on the kitchen table and nipped upstairs with the rest of the stuff.

Ten minutes later, I was up the greengage tree, lashing the nesting box into the junction where three really strong branches came together, near the top. The cables were already taped into position and ready to be hooked up. I'd attached them to the string I'd fired out of the window and hauled them across the gap to where I was now working.

The whole operation had been fiddly, especially coaxing the cables through the tangled branches but the twins took no notice. They just got on with fixing the bikes and let me do my thing. They didn't even bother to look up.

Sniff lay quietly on the path between us, waiting for his breakfast, yawning and scratching.

In the end, I had to break the silence because I needed a hand with the video camera. If I dropped that, I was dead.

'Could you give me a hand for a sec?' I said, after I'd popped into the house to collect the camera from the kitchen table. 'If I get up on that branch, d'you think you could pass this up?'

Tatty and Minta crossed their eyes and tutted and sighed to show what a drag I was. Finally Minta got up and took the camera. 'It'll never work,' was all she said. She waited while I heaved myself on to the lowest branch and stood on tiptoe to pass me the camera.

'D'you want to come up and help me get it in position?' I asked.

She tutted again, but climbed up after me. 'Now what?' she grumbled.

'Can you just hold the camera steady under the nesting box while I strap it in and connect it up?' I'd already taken the floor off the box, leaving just the walls and the roof, and then I'd tacked on a sling made out of doubled-up masking tape for the camera to rest on. Minta helped me get it in place. The lens was poking through the entrance hole, and pointed roughly in the direction of the track and the road. She looked at the mains cable and said, waving a thumb at the camera in its weather-proof housing, 'This is battery operated, isn't it? You'll wreck it if you try putting mains current through it.'

'It's got an A/C adaptor,' I explained. 'It reduces the current to fifteen volts. I'll go and turn on the electricity,' I said. 'Can you hang on here?'

'Oh, sure,' she said sarkily. 'Take your time.'

I hopped down before she changed her mind, and ran into the kitchen. Mum, Dad and Sal were zombying about in their dressing gowns, scratching and yawning. They looked surprised when they saw me coming in from the garden, fully dressed at this hour, but luckily Sniff was starving and started making such a racket that I got past them, no questions asked.

I plugged everything in, turned on and . . . fizzz. No picture on the TV monitor.

Leaning out of the window, I called across to Minta, 'Could you try to focus it a bit?' I saw her pulling the zoom-lens lever. Still no picture. By now, curiosity had got the better of Tatty. She had abandoned her work on the bikes and climbed up the lookout tree to join Minta. She leaned out dangerously so that she could get a better look at the camera.

'Shouldn't this thing be switched to MONITOR?' she yelled.

That was it! I'd forgotten. 'Brilliant!' I called. 'Give it a go.'

Suddenly, the screen brightened and I was looking at . . . twigs — the boundary hedge! 'Great! It's nearly there!' I shouted. 'Point it down a bit . . . now across . . . that's it . . . now left . . . up and . . . hold it! That's spot on. Can you strap it in position there? There's a roll of masking tape by your elbow, Minta . . . that's it, you've got it.'

I sat back on the bed and looked at the screen. There it was, large as life, no doubt about it — the track, all the way down to the tarmac road!

'What's going on?' Uh-oh, that was Dad's voice, coming up loud and clear from under the window. I peeped out. He wasn't looking too chuffed.

There was a grating sound, the twins' window just along from mind opened wide and Lolly's head stuck out of it. Dad and I turned to look at her puzzled face. Then Mum and Sal came out of the back door with pieces of crispbread in their hands to see what all the excitement was. Sniff came out as well and took a bite out of Sal's crispbread while she was looking up at me.

What else could I say except, 'Why don't you all come up here and have a look?'

Thirteen

Just as I'd expected . . . there were some BUTs.

For example: It's all very well,

BUT who said I could muck about with the video camera?

BUT didn't I realize how expensive these things are?

BUT what if it rained or the wind blew and it fell down and got smashed to pieces?

BUT what if somebody wanted to use the video camera?

Typical.

I pointed out that the last BUT was the doziest BUT of all. Nobody ever had time to use the camera for taking videos. We were all too busy doing things to want to take pictures of other people doing things. Mum and Dad had to stop to think about that one, which gave me the chance to get in the real winner about round-the-clock security and Lolly's peace of mind. That really got to them. They looked at Lolly and went all crumply round the mouth. I expect they'd suddenly remembered the panic stations on the beach and the worried conversation they'd had over the washing-up.

Most of the other BUTs were to do with whether the

camera would get damaged, and even Dad had to agree that putting it under cover in a nesting box was a stroke of genius. And when he'd finally climbed the lookout tree himself and fussed about, checking that the connections were really safe, making one or two refinements to the strapping, he said OK, he was convinced, it was a really cool system and it could stay where it was — for a trial period, anyway.

Good old Dad. First off, though, we had to have this serious chat about permission and talking things over before getting carried away with any dangerous ideas — but you could see he was dead chuffed, not only about how ace the system was, but also because there was a purpose to it and I hadn't just been fooling around.

'And great to see you and the twins mucking in together!' he said, giving me a friendly punch on the arm.

'What? Yeah, but, Dad . . .'

I didn't reckon I was getting enough credit for this, but he was off to help move the monitor into Number Two for Lolly and the girls. He dashed downstairs, got out the ladder, climbed up to my window and passed the TV set, with its wires dangling, along from my room and through to the twins, who were leaning out of their window to take it.

By then, he'd really got into the idea.

'You know, it's a pity we haven't got a thermal imaging unit,' he called up as he started down the ladder. 'Then we wouldn't have to rely on George using his lights at night, we could see him clear as day.'

'Robert!' came Mum's voice, out of the twins' window — she'd been helping with shifting the gear. She only called Dad Robert when she meant something else. Like now, she meant:

'I think we ought to forget about thermal imaging devices just at the moment, because I suspect they are mega-expensive — and besides, I think we are getting a little overexcited.'

Anyway, that's what Dad thought she meant, because he went to put the ladder in the outhouse and when he came back, he changed the subject. That's to say, he started to go on and on about what a brilliant job we'd all done on the bikes and everything.

'Great idea to get the motorbike and sidecar under cover,' he said. 'And as soon as I've done the channelling for the wiring in the kitchen, I really will have a decko at that engine. You lot have really inspired me to get stuck in!'

He stooped down to get a closer look at the bikes the girls were now working on again. 'You guys must have been at it for *hours*! Triffic job you've done, clearing up in the outhouse — and, hey! you've done wonders with these old bone-shakers! Come to think of it, I said *I* was going to help get these back on the road, too, didn't I? Not up early enough in the morning to deliver the goods, though, was I? No marks to me and ten out of ten for the gang! Brilliant job!' He gave us all a pat on the back.

Tatty and Minta were beaming — I'd never seen them smiling before.

'Yeah, well . . .' I mumbled. 'I didn't . . . er . . . It wasn't . . .'

'All this *and* a round-the-clock surveillance system before breakfast!' he went on. 'Blimey, there's no stopping you three! All you need to do now is get that old butcher's bike into shape and you're set. Then the three of you can buzz off for a ride somewhere together.'

The butcher's bike was leaning against the back wall, thick with cobwebs and dust, its tyres flat as pancakes. The brakes were locked and the mudguards were flapping loose, but the rust was only superficial and the wheels weren't buckled or anything.

'We'll soon have that sorted . . . won't we, Ben?' said Tatty. I couldn't believe it.

'Well, time I got changed, I've got work to do myself,' said Dad. He gave us the thumbs-up, clicked his tongue, and went into the house.

'Thanks,' I said, when the back door had shut behind him.

'What for?' said Tatty, still smiling.

'You know . . . about the bikes and that . . . Keeping quiet about you two clearing out the outhouse and fixing the bikes by yourselves.'

'Well, it was like your idea,' said Minta. 'And anyway, you didn't say anything about you doing all the work on the thingy.' She jerked her thumb in the direction of the wires running overhead. 'It's great.'

'But I didn't do it all,' I said.

'Anyway,' said Tatty, starting to collect her tools together.

'Anyway,' said Minta, wiping her oily hands on a rag.

'So . . . shall we have a crack at the butcher's bike?'

'Yeah, let's do it,' laughed Minta. 'I'll do the brakes . . . my speciality.'

'I'll check the chain,' said Tatty, laughing too. 'Ben can tackle the electrics.'

'Right,' I said. 'I'll see if it's got electric tyres.'

'Cheeky!' they said, and deadlegged me — *blam!* — one on each side.

*

It took the rest of the morning to fix the butcher's bike, mainly because of Sal and Sniff. Sal wanted a bike of her own.

'What about that nice orange pedal tractor out the front?' I said.

'Don't wannit!' she said. 'Dat a smelly chakta, dat wum!'

'Ah,' I said, and decided the only way to take her mind off big bikes was to let her muck about with the spanners and stuff.

OK, it was a mistake letting her have the oilcan. I just told her to hold it for me, but she ran off with it, yelling, 'I can do diss,' and started oiling the flowers outside the back door.

'Hey, Sal, that's cruelty to dumb wood calamint!' I said. 'Give it back!'

'I just do diss for a mini,' she said, without stopping what she was doing for even a second.

I knew there would be trouble if I tried to take it away from her, so I thought, fine — there were loads of flowers. It wouldn't do any real harm, letting her do it just for a minute.

That was another slight mistake because Sniff had trotted over to see what she was up to. He quite often hung about by the back door, snapping at the bees as they bundled in and out of the calamint flowers, so he must have thought it was dead interesting, the way she was poking about with the spout of the oilcan.

'No, Miff!' she said, grabbing hold of the hair on the back of his head and yanking his nose out of the flower she'd just oiled. Trouble was, that only made him more interested.

'Sal,' I said. 'Would you. . . ?'

'Just a *mini*!' she screamed.

93

'Sorry,' I said.

'Miff, dop dat,' she said. 'Bad boy! Lie down!' she poked him in the ribs with the oilcan.

'Now, don't be nasty,' I warned.

'I ticklin' him wid diss fing,' she explained, and Sniff rolled over on his back.

'Ahhh. Dere's a gooboy. I gib you tum-tum a squirt, shall I?'

'Don't, Sal!' I yelled — but it was too late. The first cold squirt got him right under the armpit and the second one caught him on the backside as he tried to run for cover.

Before I could get the can off her, she let me have it right down the front of my T-shirt, then she bit me on the hand and ran off howling to find Mum.

Mum wasn't too chuffed. She was particularly *un*chuffed when she saw my T-shirt and then, when Sniff started jumping up at her like a huge, hairy oilslick, she threw a mega-wobbly. It was going to be a heck of a job getting those stains off, she yelled, especially with no washing-machine. And somebody was going to have to catch Sniff and get cracking on him with the Fairy Liquid. And I could flaming well make myself useful, instead of putting dangerous weapons in the hands of innocent little children, and I could blinking well look after Sal *properly* after lunch.

Lumbered!

'That's OK,' said Tatty. 'She can come with us. No problem.'

'That's what *you* think!' I said.

Fourteen

'EEEEEEE!'

That was Sal enjoying herself, sitting on a cushion in a box on the front of the butcher's bike and zipping down the lane.

'WAHOOO!'

That was Tatty overtaking me on the inside with a flashy little lean and a touch on the back brake that sent gravel splattering into the roadside weeds.

'WAHEEE!'

That was Minta accelerating past me on the other side, her mudguards clanging away like a dinner bell.

'OY!'

That was me getting whacked round the earhole by Sal with the foxglove I'd given her to wave. She'd tried to chuck it at Tatty as she went past and had caught me with the backswing. And when she found out that it was funnier whacking me with a foxglove than chucking it at Tatty, she gave me another one when Minta went shooting past . . . 'OY!'

TACKATA-TACKATA-TACKATA-FIZZZZ. RRAAA-LPH-RRAAALPH-FIZZZZ.

That was Sniff galloping along the road behind and then getting fed up — and taking a short cut through the cornfield.

'Isn't this great!' yelled Tatty, shooting her legs out sideways and freewheeling round something nasty squashed in the road.

'Poetry in motion!' yelled Minta, getting on to Tatty's slipstream, shooting out *her* legs and following in tight formation.

'Butcher Boy to Red Leader! Butcher Boy to Red Leader! Coming in close on your tail! Over!' I shouted, standing on the pedals for extra push and nosing my front wheel as close as I could to Minta's clanging mudguards.

'Red Leader going left-left-left!' yelled Tatty, and she leaned in towards the nearside turn-off just before we came to a long, high stone wall.

There was a nice downhill run here, too good to miss, with a dead good ridgy surface that made your head go *gung-gung-gung-gung* and made Sal start screaming, just for the fun of getting the scream chopped up by the bumps — *eeh-eeh-eeh-eeh-eeh-eeh!*

That was why nobody took much notice of the sign where the turn-off started that said something like:

SPALDERTON HALL ONLY. NO VISITORS.
NO VEHICULAR ACCESS OR RIGHT OF WAY.

I couldn't give my old crate everything she'd got, not with Sal sitting in the box on the front, so Tatty and Minta went belting off ahead down the hill towards the bend at the bottom. I heard Tatty yelling a question about what 'vehicular access' meant, and Minta yelling back that she didn't know what she was going on about. That must have been the moment when Tatty looked back to repeat her question.

Which was why she didn't see the car coming round the corner.

What I remember next was this well hairy screeching of brakes as the car narrowly avoided crashing into the wall on the right, and the even worse sound of Tatty and her bike disappearing into the ditch on the left.

By the time Sal and I reached the spot, Minta was already thrashing through the weeds into the ditch from the road side, and Sniff was standing on the bank on the cornfield side, whining and panting, and looking down to see what had happened to Tatty.

I lifted Sal out of the box, dumped the bike and ran to see if Tatty was hurt. It all happened so quickly, and I was so wrapped up in the thought that Tatty might have done something nasty to herself, that I didn't really take any notice of the car — or its driver.

'Are you OK, Tatts?' said Minta, kneeling down and looking dead pale.

When Tatty answered, it wasn't in the voice of somebody badly injured or anything. It was more the voice of somebody trying to spit out a mouthful of ditchwater. 'Get me out of here! Yuck! It *stinks*!'

Sniff thought that sounded pretty good and dived down the bank to find out if it was *really* stinky or just a bit sort of ordinarily ditchy.

'Get *out*, you idiot dog!' wailed Tatty. 'Ben! Call him. He's trying to drown me!' She sat miserably in the shallow stream, doing her best to protect herself from a showerbath by covering her head with her arms.

Sniff didn't wait to be called. He just scrambled up the bank and shook himself all over Minta, who was trying to pull Tatty's bike clear of the ditch. 'Gerroff!' howled Minta, trying to shove him away. The more she shoved, the more Sniff bounced and shook himself. Minta was getting almost as wet as her sister, so Sal decided to show who was boss.

'Naughty!' said Sal. 'He got too thited.' She was a bit of an expert on getting too excited. She put both her arms round his neck and pulled him backwards on to the grass. It took about two seconds for most of the slime that was sticking to Sniff to transfer itself to her. After that, Sniff lay flat on his back with his legs in the air and his tongue sticking out, hoping for a good tickle on the tum. Sal squatted beside him to demonstrate how to do it.

'Can you catch hold of this, young lady?' said a man's voice. It was a deep voice, very posh.

The driver of the car was this old gent – he must have been about fifty or sixty at least. He was tall and bony, with a Roman nose, sticky-out ears and a bushy grey moustache. He was wearing sandy-coloured trousers, a white jacket and a brown trilby hat. He was down on one knee, leaning over the ditch, holding a shooting stick out for Tatty to grab hold of. He was concentrating so hard, his moustache kept turning up at one corner.

Tatty's hand appeared, and grabbed the silver handles of the stick. In two ticks, she was up the bank and standing by the side of the road, dripping wet and ponging like a drain.

'You're not hurt, are you, m'dear?' asked the old gent anxiously. He opened out the handles of the shooting stick so that they made a seat, drove the point into the soft ground and helped Tatty to sit down on it and get her breath back.

'I'm OK, thanks,' said Tatty.

'And your bicycle?' he went on.

Minta had hauled it up the bank and was giving it the once-over. 'Can't see any real damage,' she said. 'Handle-bars need straightening, that's all.'

'I say!' said the old gent. 'You must be . . .'

'Twins. Right,' said Tatty, squeezing ditchwater out of her shirt. 'But *she* wears glasses.'

'No, what I was going to say was,' he went on, 'you must be living somewhere nearby.'

'Well, not exactly,' I said. Now that the excitement was pretty well over, I'd suddenly taken in the fact that I was standing by this fantastic old car. It was an Armstrong Siddeley Sapphire in brilliant condition, probably about 1950. I ran my hand over the Sphinx on top of the gleaming silver radiator. 'We don't exactly live at —'

'You must forgive me,' the old gent went on absent-mindedly. 'I'm afraid I simply wasn't watching the road. As a matter of fact, I just turned round for a second to see if I'd left my packet of Polos on the back seat and . . . er . . . well, I must say, I got rather a shock to see you coming at me round the corner. We're not used to people on this stretch, d'you see?'

'Actually,' said Tatty, as surprised as I was to hear a grown-up owning up to something being their fault, 'I wasn't exactly looking where *I* was going either.' She opened her mouth and gave herself a quick squirt with her asthma inhaler.

The old gent wasn't listening. 'And now look at the state you're in. Could have been far worse, of course, and that hardly bears thinking about, but — my goodness! — you . . . er . . . you're all jolly mucky, what? Better do something about that pretty smartly, because — phew! I say! Rather whiffy, eh? And that goes for the littl'un and the doggy, too.'

'Dat Miff,' explained Sal.

'Yes, I know. It does, doesn't it?' said the old gent. 'Well, I think we'd better see if we can't do somethin' about it, what? Now, tell me, whereabouts are you chaps billeted?'

'Sorry?' I said.

'Where are your quarters — your mess — where are you living?'

'In some cottages over that way, not far from the village,' I explained.

The old gent's mouth dropped open. 'You don't mean . . .'

'Lavender Cottages,' Minta told him.

'Well, stap my britches!' he said, snatching off his brown trilby hat and slapping his leg with it. 'Lavender Cottages? God bless my old army boots! What an extraordinary thing! Extraordinary! I was only thinking this morning about your mother. I knocked her off her bike at pretty well the exact same spot! Amazing coincidence! Years ago now. When was that? Never mind. Down for the holidays, is she? . . . And she's got twins now, eh? And a great strapping lad! My

100

goodness, how time flies! And another little nipper, too! Well, boil my braces! Roof holding up, is it? Still, never mind about that now. Roof's not the point at this moment, is it? We're more concerned about whiffs, aren't we? Quite. We've got three charming young ladies and one . . . er . . . extremely interesting doggy standing here whiffing, and here am I, standing about gassing. Correct?'

It was difficult to get a word in edgeways.

'So what I think we'd better do is . . . er . . . did you say those handlebars are bent, young lady?'

'Not bent, exactly,' said Minta. 'They just need straightening. We can probably jiggle them back into the right position. Can you give us a hand, Ben, and hold the front wheel steady?'

'Excellent!' said the old gent. 'In that case, you two jiggle away, and if the littl'un would hold on to the doggy for a moment and you, young lady' — he meant Tatty — 'would watch to make sure that I don't reverse into the ditch, I shall turn the car round and you shall all follow me along to the Hall. My wife would never forgive me if I let you return home to your mother in a whiffy condition. Indeed no. So, gird up your loins, everyone. We shall have you all back on parade and smelling like roses in two shakes of a horse's tail. Anything the matter?'

'Did you say to follow you to the Hall?' Tatty said.

'Absolutely. It really isn't far. Less than a quarter of a mile, I'd say. You'll see it once you get up on to the top of the rise there. Won't take a tick, if you all hop on your bikes . . .'

'Do you live there?' I asked.

.

'Oh, yes, yes, quite. All my life.'

'Then you must be . . .' I didn't finish my sentence because, all of a sudden, there was this *ting-ting-ting-ting* of a bicycle bell. Sniff rolled off his back in a flash and went belting up the rise to greet the rider who was tearing down towards us from the direction of Spalderton Hall. It was a skinny kid with a long and serious face and big ears, wearing a T-shirt and a pair of pink Bermuda shorts.

'Everything OK, Uncle?' he called out as he came, and then, as he recognized Sniff — and me — 'Hey! It's you! What on earth are you doing here?'

It was Edward.

Fifteen

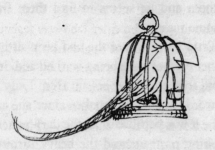

'Soldier Freddy home in beddy!' screeched the parrot.

'Can't somebody put the cover over that noisy blasted bird?' roared Lord Spalderton, leaning over from his place at the end of the long polished table to bang on the bars of the cage with the handle of an umbrella. 'Who taught him that nonsense, anyway?'

The parrot stretched its red, yellow and purple wings and flapped them so hard that the cage began to chime like a gong. Then, as suddenly as it had started, it froze on its perch and sang:

> Ning nang nong
> Crackers go bong!

Lord Spalderton reached for his brolly again.

'Now, now, Neddy, don't fuss so,' cooed Lady Spalderton from the other end of the table. 'You know very well that Edward taught him a little bit of Spike Milligan as a relief from all that Wordsworth you fill his head with. And one can get frightfully bored with daffodils and leech gatherers.'

She took a water biscuit from the plate in front of her and held it up for Sal. 'Sally,' she whispered, 'do you think you could break this into little pieces and feed it to Crackers? He does so love them and he seems to find them frightfully soothing, for some reason.'

Sal slid off Tatty's lap, where she had been sitting in her pants because her clothes were being washed and dried. She stretched up and took the water biscuit from Lady Spalderton without a word. She hadn't spoken since she came into the Hall. Maybe it was because of all the dark panelling and the serious-looking portraits and the heavy furniture, and because the rooms, like this one where we'd sat down to juice and Jaffa cakes, were as big and echoing as swimming baths, and smelt like gym changing rooms.

Tatty and Minta were pretty quiet, too. They were also waiting for their clothes to be washed and dried and were sitting at the table in things Edward had lent them. Tatty was wearing a Kaptain Amerika T-shirt and purple Bermuda shorts with hot air balloons on them. Minta was wearing Edward's SAVE THE WHALE sweater that was so long, she'd put a belt round the middle and was wearing it as a dress. The twins sipped their tea, half listening to the conversation, sometimes gazing up at the high ceiling with its chubby painted cherubs, and sometimes half turning to glance at the pictures and tapestries on the wall behind them. I could understand how they felt: it's not every day you get invited to tea by a loony Lord and Lady.

When Sal got up to feed the parrot (it was a red and yellow macaw, as a matter of fact, according to Edward), Sniff unpeeled himself from the carpet at Edward's feet and trotted off with her to hoover up the crumbs. He left a wet patch where he'd been lying, since he'd been hosed down before he was allowed inside, and he hadn't properly dried off.

Crackers saw them coming and cocked his head on one side. Sal held up the water biscuit and Crackers said, 'Earth hath not anything to show more fair — eek!'

'That's more like it,' murmured Lord Spalderton. 'The sight of some tuck seems to have put a bit of sense into him.' He turned and waved his half-eaten Jaffa cake at the wet patch on the carpet. 'Bit of otter hound in that animal of yours, is there?' he went on.

'Bit of everything,' I said.

'Damn good hound you've got there, m'boy. Takes to the water as to the manner born,' he said. 'Had no idea your mother was an otter hound fancier.'

'Well, I don't think . . .' I began. He seemed to have got it stuck in his head that we all belonged to Germ, and there hadn't been a proper chance to explain that we weren't from the same family at all.

'But I'm out of touch, d'you see. Bit old-fashioned, I dare say. I mean, I had no idea your mother had all these children. Rum old business. Here's your mother, never married, with four kiddies and an otter hound, and here's Lady Spalderton and myself, marched properly up the aisle of Spalderton church together thirty-five years ago, with the regimental band playing us in and a guard of honour to see us out — and nothing to show for it after all these years, except a parrot with very little taste in verse.'

'Don't be so gloomy, Neddy,' scolded his wife.

'Mice go *clang! Clang clang clang!*' sang Crackers, rattling the bars with his beak.

'Quick, another water biscuit!' roared Lord Spalderton. 'Before he drives us all round the bend! And Sally, take this, m'dear . . .'

Sal looked round.

'Take that for the birdie, and teach the blighter something else, would you? You teach the birdie something nice, eh?' Sal looked at Lord Spalderton as she took the biscuit and blinked. Maybe she was thinking of something the birdie might like to say, maybe she was wondering if Lord Spalderton's funny moustache was going to fall off. Anyway, she just blinked.

'We don't even get the visitors, now,' whispered Lady Spalderton seriously, picking up from where her husband had left off. She'd obviously decided not to take her own advice about being gloomy. She was very tall, like her husband, and much paler, and she was wearing a short green dress that looked like school uniform. She had straight yellow hair, with a fringe just above the eyes, purple, droopy eyelids, and a big, sad mouth. What with her whispering all the time, she looked as if she was scared the head girl might come in and put her in detention. 'We've been more or less solitary here since we closed the house to the tourists. Except for Edward, who comes to see us when he can,' she added. 'Don't you, Edward?'

'Yes, Aunty,' said Edward.

'Why don't you like having tourists to visit any more?' Minta asked.

'Like what?' boomed Lord Spalderton.

'Like have any visitors,' repeated Tatty, who was one place nearer.

'Haven't really got the heart for it. Have we, Letitia?' he said. 'Not got the heart for it, these days. Not like when we had the lavender fields, eh? By Jingo, that used to bring the cars and coaches, eh? Something special to pull 'em in — Norfolk lavender – d'you see? And what have we got now? Just a common or garden English stately home, getting rather frayed at the edges.' He took a thoughtful swig of his tea. 'Nothing to attract a crowd, d'you get me?'

'Ah, well,' said Lady Spalderton. 'Can't be helped.'

'I don't remember any lavender fields,' said Edward, screwing up his face so that it was longer than ever. 'What happened to them?'

'Drought,' said Lord Spalderton grimly. 'Not enough water, d'you see? Lavender's not a frightfully thirsty sort of chappy in the main, but he does like a drink if he's going to come on properly purply with a nice fat head on him. Not enough water, and he'll let you down. Won't give you a proper show at all. We used to have lavender fields all the way over between here and, er . . .'

'Right over to the cottages,' put in Lady Spalderton.

'That's it!' Lord Spalderton went on, waving his arm towards the window. 'Right over your way. Where the pasture is out in front there — way over to where the barley fields are. All that was lavender, once upon a time. That's why they're called Lavender Cottages, of course.'

'It was beautiful,' said Lady Spalderton. Her voice had gone so quiet now, you had to strain to hear her. 'The smell,' she said, breathing deep, filling her lungs. 'Heavenly, you know, when there was a bit of a breeze in the evenings. One does rather miss it.'

'Drought two years running, and that was that,' Lord Spalderton explained. 'The Land's so light in these parts, d'you see, it drains off like nobody's business, and without sprinklers or irrigation, we couldn't save the plants. And you can't set up an irrigation system without a reliable source of water. So that was that. We gave up the lavender business and rented the fields to local farmers — who've made a respectable living ever since, growing wheat and barley, rotated with root crops of one kind and another.'

'The really maddening thing is,' Lady Spalderton added, like someone jumping awake after they've nodded off, 'that according to Edward's great-grandfather, there used to be an absolutely splendid source of water somewhere very close to Lavender Cottages.'

'No use crying over vanished water, m'dear,' growled Lord Spalderton. 'The secret died with him, so we're finished with the lavender business, we're finished with coachloads of visitors and we shall just have to crumble away gracefully like jolly old Spalderton Hall itself, shan't we?'

'Now now, Neddy!' said Lady Spalderton, suddenly getting quite noisy. 'This is defeatist talk and it simply won't do, especially not in front of Edward. He is the heir to the Spalderton estates, remember!'

Edward jumped to his feet and raised his glass of grape juice. He stuck out his long chin and said, '*Semper Spaldertonus!*'

'Quite! Absolutely!' said Lord Spalderton, cheering up and raising his teacup. 'That's what it says on the family crest all right . . . *Semper Spaldertonus* — there'll always be a Spalderton!'

Lord Spalderton looked sort of embarrassed. He obviously hadn't meant to sound so depressed in front of Edward and a bunch of strange kids. We all felt a bit awkward, and nobody could think of what to say.

All of a sudden, the bars of the parrot's cage began to gong again. Crackers was flapping his wings with excitement. 'Bum-bum!' he said.

Lord Spalderton rose to his feet and stared at the bird. '*What* did you say?' he asked.

'Bum-bum,' said Crackers. And then he said it again.

Lord Spalderton started to laugh. He screwed up his eyes and tears splashed into his moustache.

'I telled him dat wum,' said Sal.

'Did you, m'dear? Did you? Well, I couldn't agree more. I've been talking complete and utter bum-bum. And if you ever hear me sound the retreat like that again, I shall expect to hear *everybody* telling me loud and clear to stop talking!'

Everybody joined in. 'One-two-three . . . BUM-BUM!'

Sixteen

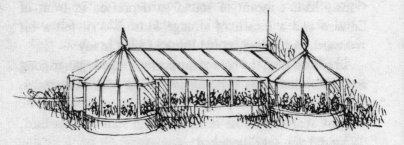

We were all out in the gardens, so at last I had a chance to talk to Edward on his own.

Every now and then, you could hear a *tokk* that sounded as if it was coming from the back of the house, but actually it was coming from the lawn on the other side of the rose beds, where the twins were having a game of croquet, making up the rules as they went along. Lord Spalderton was have a zizz in his lounger in the shade of a monkey puzzle tree. Sal was off in the distance with Lady Spalderton, chucking a tennis ball for Sniff. The garden sloped down for miles towards a long stretch of brick wall with sort of palace railings on top. Right in the middle of this was a massive pair of iron gates with the family crest and the motto, *SEMPER SPALDERTONUS*, written in curly iron letters. Beyond the railings was what they called the Park, and leading from the gates, as far as you could see, there was a wide stretch of grass, with oaks and beeches on either side. Edward had explained to me that it was called the Avenue, and in the days of the first Lord Spalderton, in seventeen something, this was the main carriageway to the house. It ran for nearly two miles from the Norwich road, and what was now the back of the house was originally the front, which explained the posh flight of stone steps we'd come down to get to the gardens.

I'd been filling Edward in on what had happened since I last saw him running for his life out of the beach car park.

'No wonder you kept making those weird signs at me when I first saw you this afternoon. Jolly good thing you did, otherwise I should certainly have let the cat out of the bag,' Edward was saying.

'I was well scared you were going to let on about getting chucked out of the phone box by old George,' I said.

'I still can't believe that great brute is —'

'Their dad, yeah!' I cut in. I explained about them and their mum hiding out in Lavender Cottages and how I'd kept quiet about George seeing me and Edward, in case they realized that George might have followed me. It would have given them all the screaming ab-dabs if they knew he might be hot on their trail again. 'I couldn't have them all panicking, could I?' I said.

"Course you couldn't,' said Edward. 'Anyway — no sign of him so far, you say?'

I shook my head.

'Just as well! Crikey, what a bruiser! I felt a bit of a rat, running out on you, actually, but I honestly thought I was going to get a mouthful of those rings of his . . . and anyway, I thought you were right behind me. Didn't thump *you*, did he?'

I said no and explained how Sniff and the lady with the beach umbrella had taken George's mind off me and given me a chance to leg it, so Edward stopped stripping bits of skin off his sunburnt nose and looked a bit more relaxed. Then I told him about fixing up the video camera in the lookout tree. He was well impressed.

'So, at least if the horrid old greaser does turn up, you'll get a bit of warning,' he said.

'You didn't by any chance see him again afterwards, did you, after you left the car park?' I asked. 'He had a motorbike parked behind . . . Remember that fruit stall on the prom at the top of the steps, yeah?'

'Yeah.'

'Well, just behind that. A Norton Dominator 650 SS, I think it was. Pretty old, anyway, and dead smart.'

'I say, was it? I do wish I'd seen it,' said Edward. 'But no, I went back to where my folks were sitting with Aunty and Uncle, and kept my head well down.'

'Where are your folks now?' I asked.

'Duty called,' Edward said. 'Got a business to run and all that. Left me here to cheer up Aunty and Uncle — quite a job, as a matter of fact, them being so down in the mouth about everything. So I'm really chuffed you turned up. And, by the way . . . er . . . what are those girls like? Better hurry and tell me, because I think they're wandering over this way.'

Edward was right. They'd obviously had enough of whacking croquet balls through hoops and had chucked their mallets down.

'Tatty and Minta?' I said. 'They're sort of OK, actually. Once you . . . so long as you don't . . . you know . . . annoy them or anything.'

'Right,' said Edward. 'Thanks.'

'Well, you want to watch it a bit,' I warned him. 'You never know where you are with those two.'

Tatty and Minta had caught up with us by the green gate that looked like a door in a church but was really the way into the kitchen garden. They were still wearing Edward's clothes.

'Hi, Edward,' they said together. It was weird the way they were looking at him. If it had been anybody else, I'd have said it was a bit gooey, a bit . . . sort of soppy. 'What's through there?'

'The kitchen garden, actually,' Edward said. 'Want to have a look? It's a bit run-down, but pretty good considering there's only Mr Morgan left to look after the whole thing.'

Mr Morgan! Of course, *he* was the gardener at Spalderton Hall. I'd forgotten that!

Edward pressed down the latch and opened the door with a smack of his shoulder.

We followed him through into this big, enclosed garden with a high wall on all sides. There were gravel paths dividing it into plots for vegetables and fruit bushes. About half the garden was really well looked after, nicely dug, with no weeds between the rows of vegetables.

All along one wall was a row of connected greenhouses, and at one end of it, winding away with a handle to crank open the skylight windows, was Mr Morgan. He waved us over.

'What d'yer reckon to them, then?' he said as we squeezed past him and into the jungly heat of the greenhouse. 'Grapes there — three different sorts; apricots, peaches, nectarines;

figs along there, look; melons in the hotbed there, in the next house along; sweet peppers . . . Oh, they keeps me outa mischief, keeping them sweet, I'll tell yer thet for nothin'! Got to give 'em plenty of air in this hot weather, thet's one thing. And proper waterin', too. Yep, reckon I could set up an' ol' stall out here and mek a fortune. 'Cept, o'course, there ain't hardly nobody round here to sell 'em to, 'part from young Master Edward.'

'Doesn't he get them free?' asked Tatty.

'Bless me, 'course he do!' said Mr Morgan. 'He's welcome to anythin' he fancies. And I shouldn't be surprised if that don't go for his friends an' all. What about one o' these 'ere peaches all round? 'Nuff juice in them, I reckon. Or try one of these 'ere nectarines if yer like, but I'd say they's a bit too firm, still.'

We all pointed out the peaches we liked the look of, and he stretched up and picked them for us. They were fat, warm and sweet, with thin skins and bright yellow flesh.

'Bootiful!' we all slurped, as the juice ran down our chins.

'What's this?' asked Tatty, picking up a stick with a bit of fur tied to one end.

'Thet? Thet's my ol' ticklin' stick, thet is!' said Mr Morgan. 'Thet pollinates the flowers, thet do. Otherwise yer don't get no fruit. Oh, there's no end of things yer got to watch. What with prunin', manurin', trainin', thinnin' an' keepin' the bugs off of 'em. Then yer got your fruitin' season, an' all thet sprinklin' an' syringin'. Thet's one heck of a job, fruit growin'.'

'Where d'you get your water from?' I asked, looking down at the snaky tangles of hose on the pathway.

'Got our own spring,' said Mr Morgan. 'Couldn't manage nothin' without it. A godsend, thet was. My brother Will, he found thet, he did.'

'I didn't know that,' said Edward.

'Oh, yes,' said Mr Morgan, 'he was gifted thet way. Proper dowser, he was. Come on wi' me. I'll show yer.'

As we followed Mr Morgan out of the greenhouse and set off at a crunching pace along one of the gravel paths, Edward gave me one of his thoughtful looks and tipped his long chin at me. I knew what was on his mind: if someone knew the secret of finding water, maybe that someone would be able to find enough up by the cottages to make it worthwhile to start growing lavender again!

Seventeen

'Don't look much, do he?' said Mr Morgan, holding the brim of his hat between his finger and thumb and scratching the top of his head. 'But thet's worth its weight in gold.'

We were peering into the dark interior of a little old shed. You could just about see a metal standpipe sticking a couple of feet out of the ground. It had a connector pipe on one side, with a control valve fitted to it, and a small electric generator with a pump, vibrating away on the other side. Mr Morgan tapped the pipe with his boot.

'Sixty-five foot down, thet's where the water was, just like Will said. He said sixty-seven, to be perfectly honest, but I reckon a couple o' feet don't lose him no credit.'

'D'you mean, he just like pointed to this spot and said, "It's down there, sixty-seven foot down . . ." and it was?' Minta said.

'Yep,' said Mr Morgan. 'An' thet keeps the house supplied and everythin'. I'm sorry I didn't say nothin' to 'is Lordship while Will was alive. But what with him bein' a bit of a Doubtin' Thomas when it came to dowsers, I didn't like to press the matter, see. 'Is Lordship thought dowsin' were all mumbo-jumbo.'

'What exactly *is* a dowser?' asked Edward, which was good, because nobody else had wanted to show their ignorance.

'Some folks call 'em water diviners,' said Mr Morgan. 'It's a gift, dowsing is. Will used to say, a lot o' folks got it, only they don't realize it.'

'How did it work?' Tatty asked.

'I'd show yer,' said Mr Morgan, 'only I ain't got the touch, see. But one of you youngsters might hev it, eh?'

He ducked into the row of greenhouses and came out holding two thin metal rods, both bent into the shape of an L. He gripped the short end in his fists, so that he was holding the rods in front of him like two pistols, and then he pulled his fists back in until they were touching his chest, one on each side. He pointed the long part of the rods straight out in front of him.

'Now, what Will used to do first of all,' he explained, 'was to start walkin' dead slow, see? Then, when he come to any water, the rods would turn in across his chest, like thet, see? Now, I'm just pullin' 'em together to show yer, but he . . . if *he* was over some water, well, he couldn't help it — them rods used to swing across all by themselves. He used to just walk like this, then he'd say "Somethin' here . . . yep . . ." And then he'd keep goin', looking for the line o' water. Thet's what they call the "aquafuir", see. Then, I'll show yer what he done. This is the bit I always used to find roight queer, like.'

Mr Morgan put his hand in his trouser pocket and took out

an old penny. He let the big old copper coin lie flat in his hand. Suddenly, he bent down and placed it on the ground. 'Say thet's where he reckon the water is, roight? Not just surface water — but a good strong source, deep down. He'd put a copper coin down like thet, he'd hold up the old rods in front of him and he'd walk from the line o' water. One . . . two . . . three paces — whatever it took before the rods crossed in front of his chest, see. Then he'd go back to the coin and pace it out in the opposite direction, and keep goin' again till the rods crossed in front of him. Then he'd say, "Thet's it! She's down there, such-and-such a number of feet down." And he was roight.'

'Was he always right?' I asked.

'Well,' said Mr Morgan, 'he was roight when it mattered, anyways. I'll never forget him driving a stake in the ground where that ol' bore-hole is now and sayin' to me, "Thet's it, brother! You get 'is Lordship to hire a drillin' team. And tell them boys to drill down sixty-seven foot. And they'll find enough sweet water to last a hundred year!"'

'Where's Will now?' asked Edward. 'You couldn't ask him to do a bit of dowsing over by the old cottages, could you?'

Mr Morgan looked sadly down at the rods in his big, dirty hands. 'Well, let me tell yer,' he said. 'Me bein' so stubborn and dull, I kept me mouth shut about what Will told me. And poor ol' Will went off up Northumberland to run his own smallholding — and not long after thet, he died. And I didn't think no more about it for a while. Then one day, about ten or eleven year ago, Her Ladyship asks me to see if I can't get the asparagus bed goin' again and I said I'd try. So I starts clearin' the weeds and I clips me scythe on somethin'. I takes a closer look — and o' course, it were ol' Will's stake what he drove in the ground there, all thet time ago. And we'd been hevin' a heck of a job makin' do with the little bit of water what the Water Board could supply, so I decided to say somethin' to 'is Lordship about what Will told me.'

'What did he say when you told him?' Edward asked.

'He said to blow the expense and give it a go! So we called in a firm from Fakenham. They come with a big ol' lorry, set up their drill and *bingo*! Thet was like strikin' oil, thet was! Water shootin' up about as high as them oaks. So ol' Will was bang on target. I only wish he'd been 'ere to see 'is Lordship's face. He didn't reckon it were mumbo jumbo when he seen thet water shootin' up out the ground like thet!'

'Can I have a go?' asked Tatty. We all wanted to find out if we had 'the touch' but she was quicker than the rest of us.

''Course you can, me darlin'!' said Mr Morgan, and passed her the rods.

Tatty didn't seem to have the touch, though she frowned and strained. Nor did Minta or Edward. Then it was my go at last — and I felt sure I'd be able to do it. Mr Morgan must have sensed how hard I was trying, because he said, 'Yer don't want to get too tense, like. Got to let your reflexes in your muscles mek them rods move, see. Will used to say he'd got this "uncontrolled suspension" in 'is muscles. Can you feel it?'

I gripped the rods until my knuckles went white, half expecting an electric shock or a vibration starting at my toes and shooting up through my body into my hands. I stepped forward, pointing the rods like some nervous cowboy at his first shoot-out. My hands were sweaty and I found it hard to hold the thin rods steady. They wandered about, pointing all over the place. There was no special feeling, no electric shock. Nothing. I was really cheesed off.

'Are you sure this is the right kind of metal?' I asked, when I saw the other kids grinning with relief that I couldn't do any better than them.

'Pretty sure,' said Mr Morgan. 'Will said yer could use anything 'cept copper. Them's galvanized steel rods yer got in yer hands, there.'

All of a sudden, we heard Sal crying, and Sniff whining and scratching at the entrance gate to the kitchen garden. The gate banged open and Sniff burst through, followed by Sal and Lady Spalderton. 'Sal was getting a bit worried about where you'd all got to,' said Lady Spalderton.

Sniff came pounding over to me, jumped up, grabbed one of the rods out of my right hand and bounced away with it. He ducked down on to his front paws when he knew he was out of reach, just to wind me up, and then as soon as I made a move, he jumped back and pelted towards the asparagus bed. When he reached the shed that housed the standpipe and pump, he shook the rod like a rat. It flew out of his mouth, right through the open door, and there was the ring of metal on metal.

'Now I'd say thet boy's got the touch!' said Mr Morgan. 'Bang on target thet were!' He raised his hat to Sniff and bowed. Sniff was so embarrassed, he turned round three times, fell over, and then rushed off to pee all over her Ladyship's asparagus.

Bang on target again.

Eighteen

Back in the dining room of Spalderton Hall, we were all set to leave.

Mrs Morgan, Lord and Lady Spalderton's housekeeper, had appeared with the clothes that had got wet and smelly in the ditch — all nicely washed and dried and ironed. Sal had her clothes back on, and Tatty and Minta went into the next room to change out of Edward's stuff.

What was great was that they had to go through this special, secret door to get to the next room. You would never have spotted it if you hadn't known about it. The wall looked like all of the others, with dark wooden panels, only, roughly in the middle, there was this long, narrow tapestry pressed behind a thick sheet of glass. And if you pushed one side of the tapestry on a certain spot, a whole panel swung inwards into another room. There wasn't a door handle or anything to give it away. It was ace.

While the twins were changing, and Sal and Edward were feeding Crackers more water biscuits, I had a close look at the way the secret door had been fitted — and that made me take a closer look at the tapestry itself. Most tapestries I've seen are dead boring, but this one, when you got up close to it, was quite interesting. All these weird little animals were peeping out from behind these bushes, and there were hunters with bows and arrows standing about five centimetres away, so that they couldn't miss if they tried. And right in the middle was this white animal — a bit like a horse or a deer — that turned out to be a unicorn. Anyway, it was lying down, it had a fence round it, and it was chained up to a tree. You could see the roots of the tree as they went down into a pool of water under the earth. And in the blue of the water, you could just make out some verses, in fancy writing:

> Weep not maidenf in diftreff
> Spalderton fhall twice [something]
> Then fhall come a double [something
>   beginning with 'f']
> And a fragrant harvefting.

'What d'you reckon all this means, Edward?' I said.

Edward came over to have a look. He screwed up his eyes, turned his head one way, then the other.

'What have you chaps spotted?' asked Lord Spalderton, wandering over.

'What does this say, Uncle?' asked Edward. 'Just here, look. There's a verse written in blue. You can only just see it.'

Lord Spalderton reached into the drawer of a nearby marble-topped desk and took out a magnifying glass. He bent low to peer through it at the embroidered words. 'Bless my soul!' he said. 'I've never seen this in my life. Right under my nose, too. Let's see . . .' He read it out:

'Weep not maidens in distress
Spalderton shall twice redress.
Then shall come a double spring
And a fragrant harvesting.'

'You can read it!' I was impressed. 'What about all those "f's"?'

'Ah, well, m'boy, that's an old-fashioned sort of an "s". That's how they used to write them centuries ago.'

'Wonder what it means,' said Edward. 'What does "redress" mean, Uncle?'

'Well, it means to put straight, set right, make up for. It certainly is most intriguing,' said Lord Spalderton.

'There don't seem to be any maidens in distress in the picture, do there?' I said.

'Ah, now I imagine that the unicorn is the maiden in this case,' said Lord Spalderton, tapping the glass with his long finger on the spot where the white animal was.

At that point, the panel suddenly swung back to reveal Tatty and Minta standing in the secret doorway.

'What's up?' they said together, tucking their T-shirts into their jeans.

'I beg your pardon. Didn't intend to hurry you,' said Lord Spalderton. 'I was just indicating this unicorn here. It's symbolic, you see — represents a young maiden. But that's about all I can tell you, I'm afraid. The meaning of the verse will have been buried with the women who embroidered this tapestry four centuries ago in the days of Sir Walter Spalderton.'

'Did Sir Walter save any maidens in distress, Uncle?' asked Edward.

'He was an old rogue,' said Lady Spalderton, who had just come in. 'And he certainly didn't save any maidens, from what I've read of him.'

'Well, it's all fanciful nonsense, no doubt,' said Lord Spalderton, 'though not without interest. Can't think how we failed to notice this verse, Letitia . . .'

He pointed it out to Lady Spalderton, who bent towards the secret door to have a closer look at the tapestry, when Crackers suddenly screamed out, 'We have lift-off! We have lift-off!' He went flapping round the room, squawking 'Bum-bum! Bum-bum!', dive-bombed the table and pinched a small bunch of grapes out of the fruit bowl. He settled for a second on a side table but had to take off again when Sniff took a galloping leap at him, knocking over two high-backed chairs while trying to get his teeth into the bird's dangling tail. All he got was one red feather and a whack from a silver tray that fell off the sideboard as Crackers screamed and flapped and went zooming off again. He orbited three times, pooping once on the clock on the mantelpiece, and once on the carpet where Sniff, if he hadn't dived for cover under a coffee table just in time, would have got splattered — and he finished up swinging on the chandelier, attacking the stolen grapes and spitting the pips everywhere.

Sal was spellbound. She was still standing on the chair she'd climbed on to let Crackers out of his cage. Her mouth was open and her eyes wide. When she realized that everybody was looking at her, she pointed up at Crackers, on his new perch near the cherub-painted ceiling, and then at the clock with black and white parrot-pooh sliding down its glass case, and she shook her head seriously and said, 'Dat not me. Wacker do dat!'

Nineteen

It was amazing that Tatty and Minta didn't kill themselves on the way home. Every time they thought about Crackers doing his dive-bombing act, they cracked up and started wobbling all over the road and crashing into each other.

'. . . And then when Sniff got hold of his tail!'

'And he went *ker-splat*, right on the clock!'

'And when Sal went . . .'

'. . . It wasn't me! The parrot done that!'

'Yeah! Wacker do dat! I couldn't believe Lady Spalderton's face!'

'It was *so* funny!'

Edward and I were riding along behind them, laughing as well. He was coming to stay for the night at Number One. Sal was showing off and getting really overexcited, bouncing up and down on her cushion in the box on the front of my bike. She started shouting her own jokes like 'SHADDUP' and 'SILLY HEAD!' and she ended up going 'KAH!' and 'FFTAH!' When she found out that saying 'FFTAH' made a big shower of spit come flying over me and Edward, she kept it up nearly all the way back home — until we got to the bend where the lane turned sharp left under the trees and the track went off to the right, through the barley.

I'd had enough of being spat on by then, so I lifted Sal down so she could run the rest of the way. We stopped for a minute to give her a chance to get ahead, and off she toddled, tripping among the weeds and potholes but with her head too full of the thought of racing us all back to Mum and Dad to care.

That was when we heard the motorbike!

We stopped breathing and just listened. Instinctively, we pulled our handlebars towards the engine noise, as though they were extra ears. It was coming from the direction of Spalderton village — and it was definitely getting closer.

Suddenly the engine revved and went up a note as the driver shifted gear to take the corner down by the junction with the main road. That was no more than two or three hundred metres away!

Without a word, we dropped our bikes on the track and dived into the barley, twins to the left, Edward and me to the right. We lay, straining our ears, bracing ourselves for the moment when the machine would come roaring to a stop among the scattered bikes. I had this picture of a big hairy fist reaching in and grabbing my hair. The pain would be my worst ever, but George wouldn't take any notice of my screams. He'd just swing me round like a hammer-thrower at the Olympics and chuck me right across the track, way out into the middle of the field.

The noise got louder and louder, then dropped as the motorbike freewheeled out of gear towards the corner. At exactly the same time, the wind got up and shook the barley, so it felt as if the whole field was shaking and whispering with nerves. Lying there, one ear on the dirt, nose pressed against a bunch of sandpapery stalks, waiting to die, I could see enough daylight to know that George only had to dismount to look down into the craters we'd made as we dived for cover, and he'd see us all curled up like scared rabbits.

But the motorbike didn't stop. It cruised round the corner of the lane by the entrance to the track and kept on going in the direction we'd just come from, towards Spalderton Hall. Just three minutes earlier and we'd have ridden slap bang into him!

Mum, Dad and Lolly had been lying out in front of the cottages, relaxing in the late afternoon sun. At least, Mum and Dad were relaxing. Lolly had been keeping one eye on the TV monitor, with its view down the track through the barley: Dad had fixed up an extension lead. She'd seen us stop of the head of the track, seen me put Sal down and watched her heading for home by herself. That was when she told Dad to expect us any minute.

Then she must have seen Edward, me and the twins diving into the barley because, according to Dad, she was up and running into Number Two before he'd got his eyes properly open, and before he heard the sound of the engine. Just to liven things up a bit, Sniff had arrived at the point where Dad had got his head together and was kneeling up, staring at the monitor. He could hear the motorbike clearly now and he was trying to get a good look at it on the screen to see whether it was going to turn down the track, when Sniff jumped all over him and smeared his sunglasses with doglick. By the time Dad had shoved him off, the motorbike had disappeared out of sight round the corner.

We stayed hidden in the barley for about another thirty seconds before we risked coming out. Then we jumped back on our bikes and pedalled down the track towards the cottages as fast as we could.

'Did you see him? Did you see him?' we panted as we reached the gate, where Mum and Dad were waiting for us. Lolly had recovered from her panic and was coming out of Number Two, running her hand through her hair and trying to look cool.

'We heard a motorbike, that's all,' Dad said. 'I didn't get a chance to get a look at the screen.' He put his hand down behind him to stop Sal from punching his backside.

'Could have been anybody,' said Mum. 'And anyway, even if it is George, Dad and I can handle him.'

'You don't know George,' said Tatty and Minta together. 'He's a real nutter when he gets worked up.'

'Listen, there's no point in us all standing here making each other nervous,' Mum said. 'That could have been anybody. If it *was* George, and he comes back, the girls and Lolly can just slip inside and we'll put him off the scent.'

We introduced Edward and explained what had happened on the bike ride. Then Dad picked up Sal and took her in for a bath. Mum and Lolly were really interested to hear about Spalderton Hall and the dowsing and everything, and they got dead worried about Tatty going into the ditch, and they thought it was a laugh that Lord Spalderton thought we were all Germ's children.

'Well, why didn't somebody put him right?' Lolly wanted to know.

'It's just as well he's still confused,' Mum said. 'Because if that *was* George, and he turns up at the Hall and starts asking questions, Lord Spalderton will be none the wiser.'

'Oh, you don't need to worry about Uncle,' said Edward. 'Once he's got an idea in his head, he's never keen on changing it.'

'And Lolly can always hide in the caravan,' said Tatty.

'Thanks, sweetheart, but I think I'll stay in the house tonight,' said Lolly. 'I've checked it out and I don't honestly see myself crawling through the undergrowth, especially not in the middle of the night.'

'Oh, Loll!' said Minta. 'After we've gone to all that trouble!'

'OK, if I'm really desperate, I'll call you and we'll all squeeze in there together. Does that sound all right to you?'

'Where exactly is this caravan?' asked Edward.

'Come on,' said the twins, relieved that somebody was taking an interest. 'We'll show you.'

Twenty

There was only one thing that prevented us getting to the hide-out.

Sniff.

Tatty was in front, crawling along the rabbit run, and had just reached the thickest, bushiest part of the secret route, when she started complaining.

'Budge out of the way!' she was saying. 'Take it somewhere else!'

'What's up, Tatt? Can't you keep moving?' Minta said.

'It's Sniff. He's wedged right on the path. I think he's trying to bury something. Looks like a hairbrush.'

'Whose is it?'

'How should I know?'

'Well, you're the one who can see it.'

'Come on, Tatty!' I called. 'Just shift him.'

'You come and shift him,' said Tatty. 'I can't get him to budge. All I keep getting is . . . ppppthhh . . . a mouthful of tail.'

'All right. Let me by, then.'

With a bit of heaving and squeezing, and the odd whack round the ear from a bunch of leaves that somebody had sprung, I managed to change places with Tatty. It was pretty dark, but Tatty was right, and by the look of the crater Sniff had dug, you'd have thought he was trying to bury himself. There was sandy dirt flying everywhere.

'Pack it in, Sniff!' I said. 'This is s'posed to be a secret pathway.'

'What's that smell?' asked Edward, who'd come up behind me through the tunnel of leaves.

I grabbed Sniff by the scruff of the neck and yanked his head round to have a look. Yuck!

'What is it? Is it a hairbrush?' said Edward.

'No, it blinking well isn't,' I said. 'It's a dead hedgehog.'

'Errr! Can't you get it off him?'

'No! He's nuts about smelly things. He'll only bite me if I try to take it. We'll have to come back later. There's no other way through to the hide-out.'

'Well, how long's he going to be?' asked Minta.

'Ages,' I said. 'It's his hobby.'

We backed out of the rabbit run carefully, so as not to open it up too obviously, and then climbed the lookout tree so that Edward could see how the video camera was fixed up.

'We should like try it out for real later on,' said Minta, leaning out of her branch to get a bit of movement going in the tree.

'What d'you mean?' I said, nearly caught off balance.

'When it's dark. We should try getting to the hide-out at night-time.'

'Yeah, we could have a midnight feast!' said Tatty. 'That'd be a laugh.'

'OK by me — but I'm a pretty heavy sleeper, I'm afraid,' said Edward, peering at the nesting box.

'Bor — ing!' said the twins together.

'I'll get you up,' I said.

'OK, then,' said Edward. He stepped backwards off the branch he was standing on and dropped like a stone.

I put my hands up over my ears and saw the twins were doing the same — which was dodgy, because once we'd all let go of what we were holding on to, the three of us nearly fell out of the tree together. We snatched at passing twigs and branches to save ourselves, and the old greengage whipped about all over the place. Meanwhile Edward was calmly dropping down from branch to branch until he reached the bottom one. There he swung his knees up, rolled over like a trapeze artist and somersaulted backwards on to the grass.

He looked up with his long, serious face.

'Anyone fancy trying a bit of dowsing round here before the light goes?' he asked casually.

Tatty and Minta looked at each other.

'Too cool for his own good,' Tatty said.

'Maybe we should beat him up,' said Minta. But you could tell her heart wasn't in it.

Twenty-one

'Come on, Edward, wake up!'

He was asleep on the top bunk in my room. I gave him a shake and shone my torch in his eyes.

'Wazzup?'

'Five past twelve,' I hissed. 'Hurry up or the twins'll think we've chickened out.'

'No porridge for me thanks, Aunty,' said Edward, still fast asleep. He turned over.

Outside, an owl hooted. It was a warm night, and with the little round window open wide, it sounded as if the owl was actually in the bedroom. Edward suddenly sat bolt upright and nearly frightened the jim-jams off me. I dropped the torch with a clatter. Luckily it didn't go out.

'Do you mind, Edward!' I said. He was always doing things without giving any warning.

He threw back his duvet. 'Get a move on, Ben,' he whispered loudly. 'It must be well past midnight.'

'Really?' I said. 'Well, blow me down.' It was a waste of time being sarky with Edward, though. He grabbed his jeans off the headboard, squatted on the side of the bed, shook the legs straight out towards the floor below, and jumped straight into them. POOM!

'Whoops!' he whispered, standing beside me.

'Shhh!' I said. 'Listen! You've probably woken everybody up!' I snapped the torch off and we stood listening. Outside on the landing, Sniff was on his feet. You could hear his claws tapping the floor as he turned round and round, and his tail thumped against something before he settled down again.

'We can't risk going downstairs,' I said. 'Sniff's bound to make a racket if we go that way.'

'Quite,' said Edward. 'Looks like a knotted-sheet job. You ready?'

I tucked my shirt into my jeans as Edward struggled with his unlaced trainers.

'Edward,' I whispered. 'We've got duvets.'

'Oh. Oh, well, never mind,' he said. He went over and crawled into the window space. 'Hang on a tick.' Somehow, he got into reverse, even though he had hardly room to move, and backed out of the window. 'Shine the torch down here,' he said.

Most people look first before they back out of bedroom windows, but not Edward. He was hanging on to the windowsill by his fingertips before he started wondering how he was going to get down. It took me two panic-filled seconds to get into position, lying flat in the window space with my head and arm sticking out over the back garden, shining the torch down into the blackness, before I remembered the ivy.

'Ah, thanks, Ben,' Edward said, and he started off down

the wall as confidently as somebody climbing down a ladder. He froze once, when all of a sudden there was a sound like a huge dog shaking itself . . . and a sparrow shot out from under the leaves. Otherwise, he made it look like a doddle.

'Drop the torch down,' he called up, when he touched ground. 'I'll show you where the footholds are.'

I shone the beam on him once more, to get a fix on his position, and flipped the torch into the air. 'Got it?' I said.

'Hands like flypaper,' he said, and flashed light in my eyes. 'Come on, back out. There's a sort of ledge a few feet down . . . that's it . . . Now let go with your left hand. Can you feel that . . . That's it! There's a thickish branch there . . .' I was off.

I was all right until I got about halfway down and began to wonder how the ivy kept its grip on the wall. That was when it started peeling off like Velcro.

'Move to your right a bit,' hissed Edward. He sounded miles away. 'There's a fixing for a drainpipe just under your foot.' I waved my foot feebly, horribly aware of the ripping sound. By the light of the torch, I suddenly caught sight of the crisscross pattern of a trellis and some twisty, knotty branches of an old Virginia creeper. I tried to heave myself sideways towards it, but somehow I just couldn't let go of the ivy. It unzipped itself from the wall some more, and down I went. It was now or never. Out went my hand, found the trellis, gripped tight. My arm was practically jerked out of its socket, but I hung on. Then something snapped. Nails shrieked as they were dragged out of the wall and winged off into the darkness. The whole trellis groaned as it gradually came away from the wall and lowered me gently to the ground, flat on my back beside Edward.

For a second I thought I was dead; either that, or somehow still floating towards the earth, a micro-tick away from being turned into tomato sauce. Or maybe I had never woken up. Maybe I was still dreaming about what might happen if I had to climb out of the window. I decided that the safest thing to do was to screw my eyes up tight and wait to see if my heart exploded.

'Hey, that was neat!' said Edward. 'I'd never have thought of that! Now where's this rabbit run?' And he was away.

I scrambled out from under my creepery covers and chased after the jumpy torchbeam towards the far corner of the garden.

'What kept you guys?'

That was Tatty. She and Minta were sitting side by side in the caravan, their round faces shiny in the light of the candles that flickered in saucers on the table.

'Hurry up and shut the door, Ben! The light!' I pulled it behind me and told Minta to keep her hair on.

'And where's your food?' said Minta.

Blast! I'd completely forgotten about food.

'I've got it,' said Edward. He pulled a flat packet out of his back pocket. 'Chocolate,' he explained, laying it on the table. 'Bit squashed, I'm afraid, but it should taste OK.'

'What a pair,' said Tatty.

'Of idiots,' said Minta.

'They don't deserve us,' said Tatty.

'They blinking well don't,' said Minta.

'Want their heads punched,' said Tatty.

'That'd sort 'em,' said Minta.

They stood up together, reached into the cupboard doors above their heads and started slapping things on to the table.

'One pack assorted crisps.'

'One pack chilled Pepsi.'

'One packet Jammy Dodgers.'

'One packet Wagon Wheels.'

'Four Kit-Kats.'

'Four snack-size Bounties.'

'One packet peanuts.'

'One packet yoghurt-covered raisins.'

'One Walnut Whip, minus walnut.'

'One apricot chew-bar with a bite out of it.'

'So what are we waiting for?'

'Let's pig out!'

'If you insist!' said Edward.

'Oink oink!' I said. And we got stuck in.

'I bet you,' said Edward, five minutes later, flicking a yoghurt-covered raisin into his mouth to join some peanuts, 'that your dad has given up the hunt and just buzzed off home . . .'

The twins stopped chewing and held up their fingers for quiet. The weird thing was that as we all sat there with our eyes swivelling about, not even swallowing, there *was* a sound. It might even have been a motorbike.

'Don't worry about it,' said Edward. 'If you're expecting something to happen, you're bound to get nervous and keep hearing things. It's just that we're all tuned in to motorbikes.'

'It's not us we're worried about,' said Tatty.

'It's Lolly,' said Minta.

'Fair enough,' said Edward. 'But even if George does come, he's got to come along the track, and if he does that, your mum'll be able to pick up his lights on the monitor. I take it you guys put the extension lead through to her room tonight?'

The twins nodded and looked a bit more cheerful, but they still held their fingers to their lips to get us to listen again.

There it was, a sort of rumbling, then a roar, then nothing.

'It's gone past,' I said.

'Shhh, shhh!' There was something else. Voices!

'Quick! The candles!' someone said and *ffft* — they were out.

'Open the door a crack. Let's listen,' Edward whispered.

'What about the smell of candles?'

'Can't be helped. Open it.'

I pushed down on the handle and put my ear to the crack. I heard someone running, a man's voice — loud — a scream. . . !

'What the heck's that?' whispered Tatty and Minta.

I closed the door and leaned on it in relief. 'It's OK,' I said. 'Don't panic. It's Sal and Dad. She must be going for a wee. I think she's tripped over, that's all.'

In the pitch-darkness, everyone let out the breath they'd been holding.

Seconds later — BLAM! — something slammed into the caravan door. The four of us hit the floor as if a bomb had gone off.

Twenty-two

BLAM!

The whole caravan shook under the attack.

'You'd better open the door,' said Tatty.

'Or he'll only kick it in,' said Minta.

He didn't give us much choice. I reached up blindly, found the handle and tugged. The door flew back on its hinges and I was knocked flat on my back.

George was not only unbelievably hairy, but he had really smelly breath. I thought he was pretty disgusting when he chucked me and Edward out of the phone box but — YUCK! — this was the pits.

'Why me?' I groaned as I lay pinned to the floor, helpless.

For an answer, I got a hot, slobbery tongue all over my face! It took a pretty sick mind to think of something that disgusting.

Sniff's.

What a relief! 'Gerroff, you stupid great lump!' I gasped.

Suddenly, it was more like being in a snake pit than in some old caravan.

'Wazzapnin?'

'Izzitim?'

'Wazzat?'

'It's Sniff!'

'Wazzeedooneer?'

'Wherezamatches?'

'Shhh! Shuddadoor!'

'Gizzatorch!'

Somebody struck a match. Somebody else snapped a torch on. Sniff sat up, blinking and panting, ready for the next game. Quick as a flash, I grabbed a handful of crisps and stuffed them into his mouth to keep him quiet.

'Edward,' I whispered. 'Edward! Keep feeding Sniff bits and pieces off the table, one at a time . . . just to stop him barking. And Minta — put that torch out for a sec. I want to take a peek outside and check on Dad and Sal.'

Ever so carefully, I opened the caravan door again. Through the bushes, I could just make out what they were saying. There was torchlight being flashed all over the place — which meant that Sal was holding the torch.

'Where Miff gone?' Sal said in a loud voice. 'Miff! Miff!'

Just for a second, the huffing and crunching behind me stopped, but then, with a newly opened packet of his favourite smoky bacon crisps rustled right under his nose, Sniff was putty in Edward's hands again.

'Don't shout, darling!' Dad said. 'You'll wake everyone up.'

'Miff wunned away,' she said. 'He det lost.'

'No, he won't. He'll be all right. He's just nosing about looking for rabbits, I expect.'

'No, he not. He wunned to da cawaban.'

'No, darling. Sniff's gone to find some rabbits.'

'I wanna see da wabbits.'

'It's too dark to see rabbits, Sal.'

'I dotta torch. I gonna go froo da bush to da cawaban!' You could hear her running towards the rabbit run.

'Yes, but that will frighten them,' said Dad. You could hear him grunt as he bent and picked her up. 'We'd better go back and find Mummy.'

'I wanna wee-wee.'

'You've just had a wee-wee, Sal. That's why we're out here, remember?'

'Wanna nuvver wun.'

'Oh, all right. Anything for a bit of peace. One more visit to the loo and then straight back to bed. Right? And no more screaming and shouting. Shall I hold the torch?'

'NO!'

'All right, all right. Shush now. Quickly, then.'

A minute or two later I heard Sal close the back door with a crash that sent a shockwave right through to the caravan. And then it was silent again. I shut the door.

'Phee—eew!' I said. 'Just for a minute there, I thought . . .'

'Yeah, we all did,' said Minta. She struck a match and relit the candles. Sniff sat, good as gold, gazing at Edward with total adoration. A trickle of drool slipped out of his mouth as Edward held up the last peanut. WUUMMPH. He polished it off and looked hopefully about for more, twizzling his ears like radio-controlled periscopes.

'That's your lot, old cocker,' said Edward. 'You've cleaned us right out.'

'What?' protested Tatty.

'You're kidding!' said Minta.

'What about my Wagon Wheel? I'd hardly started it!'

'He's wolfed that, I'm afraid.'

'Yeah, and what about my chunk of Walnut Whip?'

'Sorry,' said Edward. 'Went down the same hole as the Wagon Wheel. The price of silence and all that.'

'Well, I'm not like hanging about here with no feast,' said Minta.

'Me neither,' said Tatty. ''Specially not with Sniff slobbering all over everything. I'm going back to bed. You coming, Mint?'

'Oh, what a pity,' said Edward. 'Just as it was beginning to get exciting.'

'We've had all the excitement we're going to get for one night,' said Minta.

'Yeah,' I said. 'And that was just with false alarms. Imagine if —'

I was cut off in mid-sentence by this horrible scream. It wasn't like any normal sound. It was a sound that belonged in a graveyard, all hollow — ghostly, with a nasty echo. It was the sort of scream you can imagine making yourself if, say, you were trapped in a cave by the sea and the tide was just about to flood in over your head.

'Oh, my God!' whispered Tatty.

'That sounds like . . .' said Minta.

'HELP!' came an agonized voice from the bowels of the earth.

'It *is*! It's George!' said Tatty.

'And it sounds like he's in trouble!' said Minta.

There was no question this time of them asking me to sneak the door open. They both hit it together. I don't know for sure which one was down the steps quickest, but I do know one thing — they were both beaten to the draw by Sniff.

Edward and I jumped down after them into the clearing, and threw ourselves under the bushes and into the rabbit run. The twins had both torches, so we didn't have any choice except to feel our way along the secret path. I hadn't wriggled forward more than about a metre when something smashed me in the eye so hard that I realized for the first time what people mean about seeing stars.

After that, things got a bit hazy. I remember Edward jabbing me in the bum and asking me what the hold-up was. And I remember Sniff barking and growling just ahead. He sounded really wild. The twins were screaming at him to stop it and get out of the way. Then the garden lit up like Disneyland as every light in the house was switched on, one after the other.

Lolly's voice was shrieking from her bedroom window, 'What's going on out there? George? What are you doing to the girls? George! Don't you dare . . .'

Then I heard Dad shouting at Mum to stay in the house and look after Sal, and Sal shouting that she wasn't going to stay inside, she wanted to see what was the matter with Sniff. She must have given Dad the slip somehow, because the next thing was, we could hear her bombing towards us across the garden, making more noise than everyone else put together.

Twenty-three

If it wasn't for Sniff, we might all have been drowned.

He stood his ground, barking like mad and letting out a howl like a timber wolf every now and then. He sounded so crazy that the twins didn't dare try to get past him, and even Sal was stopped in her tracks. Which was a good thing, because she would *definitely* have been drowned.

Dad's voice was suddenly very close. 'Don't move!' he said.

Nobody moved. We didn't know who he was talking to in particular, but nobody moved and it all went very quiet.

'Give me your hand, Sal,' he said. And then he said, louder, 'Jo, can you hear me?'

Mum's voice said yes. She was still down by the cottage.

'Will you and Lolly fetch me the duckboard from the bathroom floor? Quick as you can.'

Mum didn't stop to ask why. There was something in Dad's voice that meant it was important.

Lying on my stomach, I could feel the vibrations as Mum and Lolly ran to the bathroom. Edward had his hand on my heel, just to let me know that he was behind me. I felt in front of me with my hand and found Tatty's trainer. So *that* was what had whacked me in the eye, when Sniff had started acting so fierce and stopped everybody dead. But why? What was going on?

We didn't have to wait long to find out.

'Now, careful, Sal. You come here and go to Mummy, while I help Sniff. That's it . . . Good girl!' said Dad. He was pleased, you could tell, but it wasn't over. His voice started coaxing and soothing again. 'Now let's just check this out . . . All right, Sniff. All right, boy. You stay right where you are just for a second. I'm going to slide this duckboard over . . . That's it, lift your front paws . . . Now wait. A bit more. And now you can come. Come on, boy. Over you come.'

I could hear Sniff's claws sliding and scratching on the wooden board and then I heard Dad say, 'Good boy! You made it . . .' And right away after that, he sounded dead shocked: 'Minta!' he said. 'What are *you* doing there?'

'We're all here,' said Minta, more shaky than I'd ever heard her. 'Tatty and Ben and Edward are right behind me.'

'Good grief!' said Dad. 'You don't know how near you came to . . . Now listen. All of you, listen very, very carefully. The path has caved in. There's a deep hole right in front of you. OK? Now, I've slid a board over the hole and I want you to crawl to me. Right. Careful, now. Take your time, and make your way across gently.'

I waited until Tatty started crawling ahead of me, and followed her along the tunnel of leaves. Just as I launched myself on to the wobbly board, I felt this cold draught as though I was crawling across a deep, deep grave, and a voice, weaker now but just as hollow, just as ghostly as before, rose from the depths.

'Help!'

Edward shuffled across the wooden bridge after me and we all crowded around Dad still on our knees. There wasn't room to get a proper look at what Dad could see with his flashlight.

'Is it George?' I asked, not quite sure how I should feel now that he could do no damage and his life seemed to be in danger.

Dad waved his flashlight at the duckboard. 'The ground's given way under there. There's quite a drop, from what I can make out. We said there might be a well round here somewhere. Looks as if George has found it.'

'You mean George is down a *well*!' shrieked Lolly. 'We've got to do something! We've got to get him out of there!'

'We'll get him out, don't worry, Loll,' said Mum. 'Shall I fetch the ladder, Rob?'

'We haven't got room for a ladder, with all these bushes,' said Dad. 'What we need is some rope. Trouble is, I don't think there is any.'

'There's loads of electric wiring,' said Edward.

'Not a bad idea,' said Dad. 'I've got a whole reel of coaxial cable, but it's got a plastic coating — it's too thin and slippery. George could never get a proper grip on it.'

'Not even if we doubled it up?' I said.

'We'll have to see what we can do,' Dad said. 'You know where it is. Fetch it, will you, Ben? I'm going to have a look over the edge to see how George is doing.'

I ran as fast as I could into the kitchen. As I stooped to pick up the heavy cable reel, I caught sight of something on the dresser — the four-pronged iron hook Dad and I had found among the weeds. I snatched it up and rushed back into the darkness.

When I reached the anxious bunch of people crowded round the entrance to the rabbit run, they were all straining to hear what George was saying. Dad had crawled back to pull the duckboard out of the way and he was now lying with his head over the edge of the well, shining his torch straight down. I heard George's hollow, wobbly voice, '. . . my arm. I think it's probably broken. But my crash helmet saved me from getting my head smashed in.'

'Can you touch bottom?' boomed Dad's voice.

'No way. But there's a ledge just above the water line I can grip with my good arm. Can you hurry up and drop me a rope, though . . . it's freezing down here.'

Dad turned to me. 'Did you find the cable?' He raised the flashlight and saw that I had. He also saw the grappler. 'Excellent! Just the job!' he said. 'How much cable d'you reckon we've got?'

'A lot. Hundred metres, maybe.'

'Great! We'll need all of that. We'll double it and then double it again. Hurry up and unroll it.'

I backed off and stood up with my hands through the centre of the reel while Edward and the twins tugged at the cable until it was all unrolled. Between us, we managed to double it up twice, and to pass one end of it to Dad.

It was a bit of a struggle for Dad to push four thicknesses of cable together through the ring on the grappler, but he managed it and I slid the grappler along until I reckoned it was about in the middle of the lifeline.

'D'you know how to tie a bowline on a loop?' Dad asked Edward, who was holding the other end.

Edward said yes and tied his end of the lifeline round his waist while Dad did the same with his end. The bowlines meant that the loops wouldn't tighten round their middles when they were under strain.

'OK, let's go, Edward,' said Dad, and dropping to his knees, he pushed off down the rabbit run towards the well, with Edward right behind him, gathering up the cable like so much loose spaghetti. The rest of us stood and waited, looking shadowy and scared in the light that was coming from the cottages.

'We're going to drop you a hook,' Dad called. 'See if you can tuck it under your belt or something. OK? Coming down now. Can you see it?'

'I've got it,' came George's ghostly voice, a few moments later.

'Right, hook yourself on. We're all going to pull. You just hold tight with your good hand and try to walk up the side while we pull. Let's go, Edward.'

Easing themselves out of the rabbit run, Edward and Dad stood up and began to pace backwards, slowly and steadily, side by side until they both felt the cable go taut. Without a word, I lined up with Tatty and Minta in front of Edward and we all gripped the cable, digging our heels into the soft earth like a tug-of-war team. Beside us, Mum and Lolly braced themselves on Dad's end of the cable and took the strain, while Sal, not wanting to be left out, got hold of the tail of Dad's dressing gown. Sniff didn't know what to do with himself, he was so excited. He dashed off into the undergrowth and came back with a big stick in his mouth, hoping that somebody would have a tug of war with him.

'Out of the way, boy! . . . Everybody set?' said Dad, and he waited while we all got balanced. 'Then steadily as you can . . . all together . . . heave!'

We gave it everything we'd got. At first, nothing happened. Then there was a hissing and plopping as earth and stones, disturbed by the twin cables dragging over the rim of the well, tumbled down into the water and on to George. He groaned a bit, and then slowly, painfully, like a sodden old stump being ripped out of the ground, he started to budge. We all staggered, surprised by the unexpected movement, but we recovered, stepped back carefully, held on — and kept heaving.

It probably only took a couple of minutes, but it seemed like ages before we heard George shout that he was almost at the top. That spurred us on — but by then, you could tell that everybody had pretty much used up their strength. I know I was feeling completely knackered. My hands were aching with the strain of heaving and my eye was throbbing like crazy. I had this sudden sickening feeling that we might all tumble down like dominoes and let him crash back into the water.

That was the moment Sniff chose to come and poke his dirty great stick against my legs, trying to get me to pay him some attention. 'Buzz off!' I panted.

Disgusted, he backed off down the rabbit run, dragging the stick with him.

'Sniff! Get out of there! You're getting in the way, you useless mutt,' gasped Dad.

What a time to want to muck about with a stick — just when some half-drowned bloke with a broken arm was about to drop like a stone.

The next thing we heard was: 'Rrrr-rrrr-rrrr-rrrr!' It was Sniff's special tug-of-war growl. He was tugging something all right! Just as we were ready to give up the struggle, the terrible strain of George's weight was lifted off our aching arms and shoulders and hands.

'That's it! I've got it! I've got a grip on the stick!' That was George's voice, with a new note in it, less hollow, more hopeful. 'I think I can make it now.'

'OK, everyone — one last pull on the cable,' yelled Dad. 'One, two, three, HEAVE!'

Twenty-four

'OK, OK! Stop, stop!' George sounded more like somebody yelling from under a bush than somebody yelling from down a well, and everybody collapsed like unplugged lilos among the crunchy, stubbly-cut stingers. George was up and out . . . and so was Sniff — who emerged from the rabbit run, big backside first, dragging his stick after him and still *rrr-rrr*ing.

Mum and Lolly were quickly on their feet and they rushed forward, anxious to see what state George was in, Mum trying to keep the flashlight beam steady ahead of them. Sniff turned and met them as they ran towards him. He dropped flat on to his tum and put the stick down across his stretched-out front paws. His ears were up and his tongue was waving like a big wet flag. He couldn't believe his luck that so many people were ready to muck about with him in the middle of the night! He rolled on his back across the entrance to the tunnel, whining with pleasure, as though Mum was waving some mind-numbing ray-gun at him, instead of just a flashlight. Then, as Mum and Lolly dropped to their knees at the entrance to the rabbit run, he flipped over and smothered them in hot, sloppy licks.

'Oh, do come out of the *way*, dog!' snapped Mum. 'Sniff, you can be such a pain!' She and Lolly shouldered past him and disappeared into the leaf tunnel. Sniff thought they were dead boring and came down the garden to see if the rest of us were more fun.

I wasn't looking forward to facing George again, so I was glad of the excuse to give Edward a hand with untying the bowline on the loop round his waist, and then to give Sniff some attention. I wrestled him over and tickled the trigger spot on his ribs that makes his back leg start pedalling an invisible bike. Sal came over to join in, attracted by the idea of wrestling and the chance to bite somebody.

The twins picked themselves up and followed Lolly and Mum down the rabbit run just to be near the action. Dad had gone sort of quiet. He just stood in the dark, absent-mindedly winding the cable back on to its reel.

The guy they brought out of the bushes a couple of ticks later wasn't George. I could tell that even before they got his crash helmet off, because his crash helmet wasn't a Nazi helmet — or even a big fibreglass job like the twins had. It was a World War II dispatch-rider's helmet, just like Lolly's. There was nothing Heavy Metal about him. He looked more like Biggles than a Hell's Angel, except for the jeans and the droopy football socks. When he was helped to his feet, it was obvious that he wasn't a big, hefty bloke at all — just a bit of a tub — and in fact, Lolly was taller than he was.

I turned to see Edward's reaction, and he looked as surprised as I was to hear Lolly say, 'What happened to your boots, love?'

'Had to kick them off, I'm afraid,' the man replied. 'Lost my goggles, too.'

'Can you walk?' asked Dad.

'Sure,' he said.

'Let's get your helmet off first,' said Lolly.

'Great idea,' he said. 'I feel as though my ears are stuffed full of tadpoles.' He sagged slightly as Lolly unstrapped the helmet. When she lifted it clear of his head, you could actually hear water pouring out of it.

'Come on, then, Georgie Porgy, let's get you into the house.'

Why *Georgie Porgy*? Thumped the girls and made them cry? Was this really the George they'd been worrying about all this time?

When he was sitting shivering by the stove in our kitchen, wrapped in a towelling bathrobe, anybody could see he had to be the twins' father. It was George all right. He had a round, pale face, a whacking great dimple in his chin and a lot of hair that came down in a fringe at the front of his peepy little eyes. His nose wasn't exactly squidgy but it was definitely not much bigger than a blob and it turned up at the end like the girls'. He didn't exactly strike you as looking like a poet — he was more like a librarian, really. And he didn't look like the type to beat Lolly up. But maybe that was because he was all hunched over on one side and he could only move his right arm.

One thing was for sure — it wasn't the guy in the phone booth, so Edward and I made *phew* and *wow* signs at each other, like fanning our faces with our fingernails, when nobody else was looking.

Dad was all set to drive George to hospital in Norwich so that he could get his arm and shoulder fixed, but George was just having some hot coffee and trying to get himself together. Between bouts of shivering, he couldn't stop himself grinning. 'Serves me right, really, sneaking about like that. Too blinking clever by half,' he said.

'Extremely cunning of you to sneak past our foolproof security,' laughed Lolly. It was weird. She actually looked pleased to see him.

'What security was that?'

'Ben rigged up a video camera in the tree,' said Tatty.

'Pointing down the track,' said Minta.

'Yes, and I lay awake half the night watching the monitor in my room. So how come I didn't see your lights? You were on the Norton, I take it?'

'And how did you know like where to find us?' said Minta.

'Yeah, that's what I want to know!' said Tatty.

'Hang on, hang on. One at a time,' said George. 'Give me a chance! Wow, security cameras, eh? You must have been serious about avoiding me.'

Edward suddenly jumped up as if he'd been stung. ''Scuse me a sec,' he said. 'Er, Lolly, would it be all right if I take a quick look in your bedroom?'

Lolly looked a bit mystified. 'Help yourself, Edward. The front door's not locked. But —' Edward was out of the door before she could ask him why, with Sniff hard on his heels.

'I'll tell you how I found you,' said George. 'After I'd lost you — d'you remember you shook me off at those lights on the Dover road somewhere, Loll? Yes? — Well, I went home thinking I'd blown it and I'd never find you. But the following morning, Mike Burstall, the big ginger guy, deals in antiques, remember? — Well, he rang me up to say that he'd seen *me* tootling east up the M11 towards Norwich on a 1955 BSA Gold Star with a sidecar, which reminded him that he knew a bloke in Kings Lynn who would pay a fortune for a combo like that. So I thought to myself, there can't be many '55 Goldies with sidecars on the road, so the chances were, it was you and the girls. Then I tried to think who we know in Norfolk, and I remembered Kevin used to have a cottage up in those parts. So I went through the address book, found his London number, rang it. It was sheer chance, but the lady who cleans for him was there — and told me that he was on his way to Indonesia for three months, to do some research on rice-growing. And as it happened, just before he left, she'd seen him having a heart-to-heart with an upset lady who had twin girls with her. So I thought *aha!* The rest was down to sheer detective genius.'

'The cleaning lady told you the address, I bet,' said Lolly.

'No, not quite — but I must admit she told me what village it was near,' smiled George. 'So, anyway, I sat about for a couple of days wondering, shall I, shan't I? You were so hopping mad when you left, I thought you'd never believe me, even if I came and told you, so —'

'Believe you about what?' interrupted Lolly, sharper now.

'About the black eye and everything.'

'You whacked me one right in the eye! That's all I know!' Lolly yelled. 'Look, I've still got the bruise!' She swung round to show everyone her black eye, saw mine, which was closing up nicely, pointed to it, and shouted, 'It was just like Ben's when you first sneaked up on me and slammed me one!'

'Er, maybe we ought to, um, put something cold on that, Ben,' said Dad. Things were getting a bit embarrassing and he wanted an excuse to buzz off but I wanted to stay. Besides, I didn't want to waste my first really proper black eye by soothing it too much. I wanted photos of this to show Thurston and Max when school started again — and I certainly didn't want to miss the interesting bit about how Lolly got thumped.

'I didn't sneak up, and I didn't thump you,' said George.

'Don't be ridiculous!' said Tatty.

'Come off it, George!' said Lolly.

'Like do us a favour, George!' said Minta.

'OK, I'd been giving you a hard time, yelling at you, starting rows — I admit it. I was depressed. It was getting to me that I couldn't write, it's true. But I didn't thump you. You were asleep on the couch in the sitting room, right?'

'Right. We had a row, you went off somewhere in a blazing temper. I dozed off for a second. The next thing I know — *wham!* — you'd punched me right in the eye.'

'It wasn't true. It was Wordsworth,' said George.

'What?'

'The Complete Works,' said George. 'It fell off a pile of books I'd stacked on the mantelpiece.'

'Are you trying to tell me. . . ?' Lolly stuttered.

'I tried to tell you at the time, but you wouldn't listen. You went dashing upstairs yelling blue murder and I couldn't get a word in edgeways! Next thing I knew, you and the girls were on board the combo and apparently heading for Dover.'

Lolly opened her mouth and closed it again.

'Listen,' said George. 'I finally realized while I was steaming round the neighbourhood, furious with you, furious with myself, that I had to do something to get writing again. I thought if I could just get my head together — find just one idea, even — then things would sort themselves out. So I started going through all the books in the garage and came across a whole pile of poetry books that we bought at an auction once and haven't even looked at. So I thought, that's it — simple — read! Stock up the old imagination. So I hauled out an armful and brought them into the house. You were asleep on the sofa. I tiptoed round you, piled the books on the mantelpiece and went out to get some more. I came back, saw the books tottering over, yelled at you, rushed over to try to stop them falling on your head — but was too late . . . Must weigh a couple of pounds at least, a complete Wordsworth . . . So that was it, really.'

Edward had come back into the kitchen in time to hear all this. Sniff followed him in, padded over to his dish and went slap-slap-slap at the water in it. That filled the awkward silence that followed George's explanation, and then Edward said, 'I've found out why Lolly didn't see your lights on her monitor . . . The camera was pointing the wrong way. It must have happened when we were all swinging about in the lookout tree while we were planning our midnight feast.' I was glad the system hadn't failed because of some technical problem.

Sniff stopped slapping and curled up on the warm stones by the stove. He looked up at George, wrinkled his head while he worked out who he was, remembered, put his chin down, huffed at the ashes and shut his eyes.

'Brilliant dog, that,' said George. 'I think I'd have been a gonner if he hadn't given me an extra pull with that stick.'

So that's what all that *rrr-rrr-rrr*ing was about! Mum and Dad and I looked at each other and then at Sniff . . . and we all decided at the same time that it would be a shame not to let George carry on thinking that the daft old bathmat had a brain!

Mum was dead chuffed to think that somebody apart from us might have a soft spot for Sniff. You could tell, because she didn't go bananas about the midnight feast. 'Oh, it was a midnight feast, was it?' she said, winking at Lolly. 'I suppose it had to happen sooner or later.'

'We heard a motorbike coming down the lane from the village late this afternoon,' said Dad. 'Was that you, by any chance?'

George started to nod but stopped himself because it hurt. 'Yep, that was me,' he said. 'I noticed the track but didn't see the cottages because of the trees. I just kept going. Ended up at a place called Spalderton Hall, as a matter of fact.'

'Did you meet Lord Spalderton?' Tatty asked, grinning at Edward.

'Yes, I did. He was the guy who gave me a clue about you being here. It was a bit confusing, but he thought there was a lady called Germ who had lots and lots of children including twin girls, so I thought there was a chance he'd got it mixed up and the twins might be Tatty and Minta. Interesting bloke, though — knows a lot about poetry. We had quite a long chat, actually.'

'Well, if Lord Spalderton told you we were here, why didn't you come over while it was still light, instead of sneaking up in the dark?' Lolly asked.

'Sorry about that,' said George. 'It was stupid of me. But the fact was, I felt such a fool. I thought it would be best not to turn up and risk another row. So I decided to wait till late and have a poke around — see if I could find the combo or something that would confirm it was you and the girls. If it was, then I planned to contact you — sent a postcard or something — and see if you were still fuming at me. So I drove over to Fakenham, found a pub, had something to eat and hung out there until after eleven. Then I drove back here — got here about midnight.'

'What did you do with the Norton?' asked Lolly.

'Left it in the lane,' said George.

'We heard you!' I said. So did Tatty and Minta and Edward. Mum said to shush or we might wake Sal, who had dropped off in Dad's arms.

'We heard you in the caravan,' said Tatty.

'So I discovered,' said George. 'I'd just had a look round the side of the house — still couldn't see the combo or anything — when I heard voices. It was the little girl talking to her dad . . .'

'Sal,' said Minta.

'Right,' said George. 'Anyway, I heard them talking about a caravan but there was no sign of one. Well, then the little girl — Sal — ran over and waved her torch under some bushes, so I figured it must be around there somewhere. I waited until Sal and your dad went back indoors and went to take a look for myself — I had this little pencil torch, you see. I got to the bushes and I heard voices. I was pretty sure I heard Tatty and Minta but I wanted to get close enough to make sure. I got right down, found the pathway under the bushes, and started crawling along it. I must have gone about three or four metres and — that was it! The ground just opened up. I really thought I was a gonner.' He started shivering violently.

'I really think you ought to get George off to the hospital, Rob,' Mum said, taking Sal from Dad.

'Are you feeling up to it now, George?' asked Dad.

George said yes and Lolly got up and pulled on a sweater. It was a warm night but George's shivering had got to her.

'We're coming too,' said Tatty and Minta.

'Better not,' said Dad. 'It's been a long night. You need to get some sleep.'

'I not tired,' came Sal's voice.

Sniff twitched and bumped his nose on the leg of the stove when he heard her, but neither he nor Sal had the energy to open their eyes.

Twenty-five

The following morning, I woke up thinking I was in a tent. It turned out that Edward had stuck his Chicago Bears baseball cap on my head while I was asleep, and Blu-Tacked a note to the peak.

The note said:

Dear Ben,
Good laugh last night. Gone back to S.Hall to ask Uncle something. Back later.
See you, Edward

PS The eye is looking dead good. I'll fetch my camera.

Dad was looking a bit bleary when I saw him. He said they were keeping George in hospital overnight for observation. He'd busted his collarbone, he was badly bruised and suffering from shock.

'D'you think I should have gone with you — shown them my eye and everything?' I said, while Dad kicked among the nettle stumps under the greengage tree.

Dad gave me a do-me-a-favour-son look, which I thought was a bit unfair. So I said, 'Because we were dead shocked, too, you know — what with Sniff hammering at the caravan door like Freddy from "Elm Street" and then hearing George screaming his head off.'

Dad kept scraping around with his foot. Something was tickling my neck. I scratched it.

'And the twins were really really scared . . . You know what girls are like. They'd probably have dropped dead with fright if me and Sniff hadn't . . .' That fly or whatever it was was really getting on my nerves. I flapped with my hand to get it away. Immediately I wished I hadn't.

I could tell it was something horrible, just by the first touch. With a horsefly or a wasp or something that size, sometimes you're lucky and you can swat them away before they get their stingers into you — but this was bigger. I only grazed against it with the back of my hand, but even then I sensed that this thing was soft and squashy, covered in a nasty soft fuzz. I ducked away, thrashing about with both arms, shaking my head, yelling, but the thing was tangled in my hair, riding there, trying to sink its poisonous fangs into my scalp. Desperately I clawed it away from my head. It was the biggest, greasiest, blackest-looking spider I'd ever seen outside a zoo. As it swung on its thread, you could even see the moisture on its eyes and the individual hairs on its crawly, disgusting legs . . .

'WAAAAAH!' I dropped down so fast I bit my tongue.

'What the. . . !' said Dad, spinning round.

'Shame,' came a voice.

A voice? I couldn't work out where it came from.

'Yeah, shame.' That was definitely Tatty. Or Minta. Where were they?

'Dropped dead with fright, didn't he?'

'Nothing we could do about it, was there?'

'Thought he said he liked spiders.'

'Only a boy, though, wasn't he?'

'What could you expect?'

'Allergic to spiders, probably.'

'Yeah, even ones on elastic.'

'Yeah, free with Rice Krispies.'

'Good thing we had him to look after us in the nasty caravan, though, eh?'

'Yeah. Otherwise we'd have gone all soppy, wouldn't we?'

'Oh, do belt up, you two,' I said, picking myself up. Tatty and Minta, both wearing jeans and yellow and red striped sweaters, were stretched out in the branches of the lookout tree above me, grinning down like two Cheshire caterpillars. Minta was dangling the toy spider.

'Pinged up, I'm afraid, old son,' said Dad.

Tatty and Minta started to climb down, dead chuffed with themselves. 'What you looking for, Rob?' they said to Dad.

'Yeah, Rob, what you looking for?' I said. Dad swung his foot at my backside but I dodged out of the way just in time.

'I'll get you for that later, cheeky,' Dad laughed. 'And I'm not looking for anything. I've found it,' he said. He bent and picked up the grappler from under a bush. 'It came off the cable when I wound it in last night. But now that it's turned up again, maybe we can do a bit of fishing with it.'

'Fishing for what?' said Tatty, dropping on all fours out of the lookout tree.

164

'Sharks, by the look of it,' said Minta, landing beside her.

'I was thinking more along the lines of your father's boots and goggles, actually,' said Dad. 'But you never can tell what you'll find down a well . . .'

'Wow — another poet! Wouldn't you know it!' teased Tatty. Then she suddenly turned her head — flick — like the rest of us: there were cars coming down the track.

We didn't have long to wait before we discovered who our visitors were.

'Well, well, well!' came a loud voice from back near Number Two. It was Mr Morgan, closely followed by Lord Spalderton. 'Sorry about thet — thet's a terrible old joke!' said Mr Morgan.

'And sorry to call on you unannounced,' said Lord Spalderton. 'I'm afraid you must blame me for that, Sir.' He stepped forward with his hand held out. 'Spalderton's the name.'

'Moore,' said Dad. 'Robert Moore. How d'you do?' He shook Lord Spalderton's hand.

'How d'you do,' said Lord Spalderton. 'Hope it's not inconvenient, but my nephew tells me that a well has been discovered. I simply had to come and see for myself.'

'Your nephew? Ah, you mean Edward?' said Dad. 'Where is he?'

'Here,' said Edward. All of a sudden, there he was, pointing a camera at us from the dock leaves at the end of the rabbit run. 'Say Cheddar.' The camera clicked and he scrambled to his feet.

'Edward! Where did you spring from?' said Dad, dead surprised — as we all were.

'Old Indian trick,' explained Edward. 'Now come on, Ben. One nice close-up for the friends back home.' Click.

'By Jingo!' said Lord Spalderton. 'That's just about the finest shiner I've seen since I was at Harrow!'

'Ah, well, you didn't see Loll's,' said Minta.

'Yeah, that was even better,' said Tatty.

'Like all bloodshot where the white normally is,' said Minta.

'And sort of greeny-purple underneath,' Tatty added.

'Really?' said Lord Spalderton. 'Yes, I should like to have seen that. Even so, this one is jolly impressive. Now tell me,' he went on, 'am I right in thinking that the well is in there somewhere?' He pointed down the rabbit run that Edward had just popped out of.

'That's it, Uncle,' said Edward. 'I've just been to check it out in daylight. But what with the leaves being so thick there, it's frighfully tricky.'

'I say, d'you think there'd be any objection to our clearing the undergrowth so that we can get a better idea of what exactly has been discovered here?' Lord Spalderton said to Dad.

'Well, as you know, I'm not the tenant,' said Dad. 'Germ is . . .'

'Now then, perhaps you'd be so kind as to explain who exactly is who here,' said Lord Spalderton, twizzling his moustache in a puzzled sort of way. 'My nephew has been trying to explain who all these children are and who that delightful chap on the motorbike was who dropped in yesterday after the children left. But I have to confess, I'm still somewhat confused. And what has happened to young

. . . young Sally. And that most amusing Otter Hound?'

It took Dad a fair while to straighten out Lord Spalderton because he was still stuck on the idea that all us children were Germ's. Still, Dad finally managed to explain about Mum and Lolly and who they belonged to and how they'd gone to Norwich to collect George from hospital and taken Sal and Sniff with them.

Finally, Dad said that he thought Germ would want the shrubs and bushes cleared from round the well, in case any of her children or their friends forgot about the hole and tried to get to the caravan, so Mr Morgan fetched his chain-saw from the back of his Morris Traveller and started the job.

It didn't take long for him to zap everything that was in his way and soon we were all looking at the hole George had fallen into. Mr Morgan lay flat on his stomach and gazed down.

'I suppose there's no doubt that this is the well my grandfather was referring to?' asked Lord Spalderton.

'I reckon thet must be, Sir,' said Mr Morgan. 'All very nicely shored up with stone, too — except at the top here, where the stones have tumbled in. But I'd say thet's somethin' you could see to without too much trouble. Smells pretty sweet, too, I'd say.'

'I wonder. . . !' Lord Spalderton had gone all red in the face and his ears that stuck out like Edward's went scarlet with excitement.

Edward was pretty charged up as well. 'It's like what it says in the tapestry in the drawing room at the Hall!' he said. 'A double spring! I get it now. It's nothing to do with seasons; it's to do with water . . . one spring in the walled garden and another one here. Do you see?'

'Bless my soul!' shouted his uncle. 'How does the rest of the verse go, now. . . ?

> 'Something . . . maidens in distress
> Spalderton shall twice redress.'

'Now, I wonder what maidens my grandfather rescued . . .'

'Not your grandfather, Uncle!' said Edward. '*You!*'

'Nonsense!' blushed Lord Spalderton. 'When have I ever. . . ? I mean, I'm not the knight in shining armour type!'

I suddenly twigged what Edward was driving at. 'Germ!' I yelled, jumping up. 'You pulled her out of a ditch and gave her somewhere to live!'

'Bang on!' said Edward. 'That was the first maiden. And the second one is the charming young lady on my left — Tatty! Surely you haven't forgotten that you rescued *her* from a ditch? That was only yesterday.'

Lord Spalderton's mouth was wide open.

'You see, Uncle? It was nothing to do with charging about on a big white horse, rescuing maidens from dragons and castles and stuff,' said Edward.

'More like charging about in an Armstrong Siddeley Sapphire, pulling young ladies out of ditches,' I said.

'So you see, Uncle, it's all a prophecy,' Edward insisted. 'A Spalderton *did* rescue two maidens and two springs have turned up. So who knows, maybe the rest of the verse will come true . . . only I can't quite remember what the rest of it was, apart from the double spring bit.'

Lord Spalderton obviously had a better memory for verse than for who was renting his cottages. He could remember it word for word:

> 'Then shall come a double spring
> And a fragrant harvesting.'

'And there ain't nothin' fragranter than what lavender is,' put in Mr Morgan, up on his knees now and slapping the dirt off his hands. 'And I'm willin' to bet that this 'ere well would get yer all the water yer need to get them lavender fields goin' properly.'

'Do you really think so?' gasped Lord Spalderton. 'By George, wouldn't that be something!'

'By George is right,' said Dad. 'George being the name of the twins' dad, you see? And he was the one who found the well, really.'

It was the twins' turn to blush.

'I wish I could find a way to thank him,' said Lord Spalderton. At that moment, we heard the familiar sound of the Passat coming down the lane.

'That's probably my wife bringing him back from hospital now,' said Dad. 'But if you don't mind, I think I'd better concentrate on getting some sort of covering over the well, temporarily at least. I'd hate Sal or Sniff to fall down there.'

'Why not leave thet to me, Sir?' said Mr Morgan. 'I've got me tools and plenty of wood in the back of me wagon.'

'Thank you, Mr Morgan,' said Lord Spalderton. 'I think that's a splendid idea. Then everybody can come back to the

Hall with me. It would be a great pleasure for my wife and I to be able to talk to you all together.'

Twenty-six

'Snap! the trap flipped
Hand grabbed
Ungripped
And over
And over
Into the
Wet smacking
Bone-snapping black.'

'Fine work, George, deeply felt!' said Lord Spalderton.
'Damn good.'

'Thank you. That's very kind of you,' said George,
shutting his notebook with his good hand. The other one was
tucked into a sling. 'Not exactly Wordsworth, I know, but
I'll tell you something. I'm beginning to feel — I don't know
— unblocked. My head was spinning in that hospital bed. I
had so much to think about. Now all I want is to go
somewhere quiet and write it all down. It's a heck of a relief,
I can tell you.'

'Yes, for all of us,' said Lolly, with feeling.

'And you think that what triggered this inspiration was falling down a well?' whispered Lady Spalderton anxiously.

'Yes!' agreed George. 'I suppose it was what you might call a new source of inspiration . . . after all, a well is a source . . . a spring — d'you see what I'm getting at?'

'The verse in the unicorn tapestry said there would be a double spring,' said Edward. 'Maybe that's what the prophecy meant.'

'Good Lord, what a fascinating thought!' exclaimed Lord Spalderton.

Tatty and Minta didn't think there was anything fascinating about this stuff. They'd eaten two slices of Mrs Morgan's cake, taken a long look at the famous tapestry, watched Sal feed water biscuits to Crackers, and stood by the big french windows, looking at Sniff chasing plovers off the lawn down by the gates to the Park. By this time, they were well cheesed off.

When Lady Spalderton started going on about how brilliant it would be, now that it looked as if they could replant the old lavender fields, and attract more visitors to Spalderton Hall, Tatty and Minta started picking the paint off the window frames. You could tell that if things got any more boring, they were going to start nibbling the putty like a couple of hamsters trying to get out of a cage.

'Would you ever consider a post as poet-in-residence, if Lady Spalderton and I were to establish a summer course for writers?' asked Lord Spalderton. George nearly fell of his chair with excitement but the twins were so desperate to get out, they asked if Edward and I would like to go and muck about outside. And when we said no thanks, they were even prepared to take Sal for a little walk down to the walled garden.

Sal didn't need asking twice, so they were off down the steps and across the lawn by the time Lolly came up with her idea: 'It's just a thought,' she said, 'but while you're on the subject of putting the Hall back on the map — have you ever thought of vintage car and motorcycle rallies? George and I have plenty of contacts among British classic bike enthusiasts, and you obviously know a thing or two about classic cars, judging by the condition of your Sapphire . . .'

Edward's loony old uncle and aunty thought that was such an incredibly ace idea, they rang for Mrs Morgan and asked her to bring some champagne.

For a little while after that, there was a dead interesting discussion about whether the BSA Rocket Gold Star was much of an improvement on the A10 Golden Flash — and stuff like that. Dad said he knew a bloke who had restored a Royal Enfield 350 Bullet and he reckoned it was pretty oil-tight, so long as he stuck to thick oil, like Castrol GP. Then Mum said she used to go out with a bloke who was secretary of the Panther Owners Club, and Dad went pink . . . In fact, they all started looking a bit pink and talking dead loud, so Edward and I went and sat on a side table and thought about what we could do with what was left of the holiday.

Edward poured out some champagne for us, but it didn't taste that good and it was too fizzy, so we gave it to Crackers, who seemed to like it. He only had three sips, and he did a whole long verse about a highland lass singing in the fields.

'Cheers, Crackers!' called Lord Spalderton.

'I'll drink to that!' called George, and they both went back to their conversation.

'Must have been Wordsworth,' said Edward. 'Can't see much in it myself. Fancy a cigar or anything?'

I said, 'No thanks. But you go ahead. You'd better have a practice if you're going to be rich.'

'Well . . . maybe later,' said Edward. He looked at Mum and Dad and Lolly and George and Lord and Lady Spalderton yacking away like crazy, and he pulled a bit of skin off his ear. 'I've been thinking,' he said.

'Oh, yeah?' I said.

'Now that Uncle and Aunty have decided not to let the Hall just crumble away, right?'

'Right.'

'And now that I'm probably going to be mega-rich, right?'

'Right.'

'And all because of the well, really.'

'Yeah. I s'pose so.'

'OK, I'd like to do something really special for the Discoverer of the Well.'

'That's great, Edward,' I said, 'But your uncle's already talking about getting him to run a summer school and fix up some rallies and that. I don't see —'

'I'm not talking about *George*!' said Edward.

'Who, then?' I said.

'You mean you haven't worked it out?'

'What are you talking about?'

'Who excavated it and covered it over again? Who buried a squashed hedgehog right on top of it?'

'Wow — of course!' I said. 'That time we couldn't get

174

through to the caravan, because he was in the way! That's what he was doing, wasn't it? Sniff! He must have weakened the covering by digging almost through to the well-shaft — and then George's weight did the rest!'

'Shh—shh!' said Edward. 'I don't want the others to hear, not yet anyway. Grown-ups always get to give out the rewards and that's not fair. *I* want to give him something. So come on, you should know. What would he really, really like?'

I thought about doggy chocs, bones, hazelnut spread. Sniff was crazy about them all, but none of them was really special, and I knew it was important to Edward to choose the right thing.

Finally, it came to me. 'It's got to be a squashed hedgehog,' I said. He is *crazy* about smelly things.

'If you say so,' said Edward, frowning with concentration. 'But where the heck are we going to find one?'

'Get your bike,' I said. 'Let's get Tatty and Minta. And we'll have to take Sal, I s'pose.'

'Why? Where are we going?' asked Edward.

'Back to the well,' I said. 'George must have dragged the hedgehog into the water with him when he fell in, so it's bound to be down there still. We'll hook it out with the grappler — and see if we can find George's boots and goggles while we're at it. We'll have to get a move on, though, before Mr Morgan nails down his new cover for safety.'

We jumped down off the side table and slid out quietly through the french windows. The grown-ups were still laughing and nattering away.

We whistled to the girls, who were over by the monkey

puzzle tree, chucking croquet balls for Sniff to fetch. He looked round to see if I was calling him, not that he was going to take any notice so long as there were croquet balls to chase and chew.

'Whatja want?' yelled Tatty and Minta.

'Bum-bums!' yelled Sal, and jumped up and down blowing dribbly raspberries.

'We're going fishing for hedgehogs!' Edward yelled back. 'Coming?'